I0713787

ko yo te, 1st edition

first published 2023 by rain of long time

copyright © 2023 by ageha

a complete digital version of this book can be downloaded, free of charge, from:

https://rain-of-long-time.com

made using free, open-source technologies, including Vim, X$\exists$T$_{E}$X, Scribus, GIMP, Krita, and fonts released by The League of Moveable Type

ISBN: 978-1-7351101-2-7 *paperback*
ISBN: 978-1-7351101-3-4 *pdf*

KO YU te

a Novel
by
ageha

むねの清水
あふれてつひに
濁りけり
君も罪の子
我も罪の子

与謝野 晶子

As you go through the Difficult Place
The strong snake-shadows shall bind you
Under the ashes of Space
Ah, never look back, run Fast
—Stella Benson (破片)

For 熊猫

fe

there is a city. it is vast and it is empty
i talk about it with my boyfriend. i show him pictures
"広ーい！！", he says. "there's no one!"

.　　.　　.

there is a house also, and it is purged of dust and clutter
keepsakes are thrown away, and in their place is stored anxiety
and want

"what a high ceilings..."

.　　.　　.

the house, you left behind you and you somehow stayed alive.
you ate spinach and rice and drank left-over beer, and your
body began to dwindle so that the you drained out of you at a
rate that couldn't be replenished

but you tried

ff

you live in a box, on a plate on a ball in a well

nearby there is an empty lot, where sometimes gangs will leave discarded carcases, of people who were somewhere they should not, have been, had been, were done and gone

the church across the street has food, but it feels too imposing, going over, taking things, when there are families around you, and you wait it out and find that eating can be more a luxury than *How Your Body Works* had said it was, once ago, upon a time

•　•　•

you are better at it these days, being alone

•　•　•

sun comes up and sun comes down (and all the world is round around)

living with the human beings in the human town

difficult to smile sometimes. pulled into a frown

time to get away, time to take a day to try and find what was it,
ah, but you've forgot again, fen, furrow-bog of feelings, falling
in, wait the sun comes down again and we can get away to
notherday. across the wall of sleep

. . .

you work weekends at the library, shelving books and helping
people find the things they're certain that they really do not
want, and no i said ○○; can't you hear me what i'm saying?
and it's oh

oh yes, that's it

the library is not a place of *calm* any more. all the books have
gone away, making space for old computers and this gaping
emptiness, and all you want is to get lost again, between the
tower shelves, and smell that smell of moulding paper mixed
with glue that takes you back to times before, when you were
small and still-alive

子

OO

you remember once, when you were small and still-alive, there was a contest at the local pool for guessing "how many goldfish crackers are in the goldfish bowl?", and you looked to see how densely they were packed, and then you calculated, multiplying that against the volume of the cylinder, and later, when they called your mother up to say you won, it felt like somehow you had cheated, like this sort of empty feeling in your chest, and then you wanted it to be that it was someone else who won, but that's not the way it went

.   .   .

later, swimming, after, with the pool all to yourselves. the tickets that you won, and it's just you + family

the pool is soon to be closed down, probably because this is a neighbourhood for olds and all the olds have pools their own, or else they do not care for swimming or have grown too old, to show their bodies out in public places, hiding from a world that's filled with youngs like you who do not have the decency, to leave them be and to their peace

lane flags flutter in the breeze. bleached pastel and brittle

you splash. you run. you make a lot of noise, and you are
young

and you are bored

the sun is turning slowly, and you turn along its path. you try
your best to float but can't quite manage, as your legs have got
no fat and they keep sinking, and you hold yourself with air,
blow your lungs way up as far as they will go and tilt your head
way back so that it feels a little like you're balancing on one
of those exercise balls, one of those exercise balls, one of those
exercise balls that you've seen on tv, and that they once had
had at a neighbour kids' house, you went because of church-
group-things, and there you are, your spine stretched taught,
and blood runs to your eyes and tips-of-ears, and hanging with
your hair just barely brushing at the ground, and all the room
is filled with upside-down and people holding magic paper
plates that, even upside-down, will grip their contents firmly,
keep the beans and unripe watermelon firmly in their place,
and if you stop to listen closely you can hear, just out the door
and round the corner, someone starting to complain because

it's meant to be a tournament, and you guys just are playing on your own and that's not the way it works, and there behind them, out beyond the pingpong table, through the gate and round the back to where the lighting doesn't reach, there is a fainter creaking sound, shudder sigh of swinging chains, where back-and-forth and push-and-pull and periods and amplitudes are trying hard to help a pair of little people to forget that soon they'll have to face each other, faces burning red, a red invisible to now scotopic vision, vision dimming as the sun is dragged behind the granite hills

this is the story:

on monday nights, my mother leaves me at the library. she comes to pick us up at school, usually well after everyone else's families have come, and then we'll go to sprouts for some non-perishables, or else to the dollar store or the expired food store, where they take all the food from grocery stores that's past its sell-by date.

sometimes we'll go to mcdonalds because of the dollar me-nu, but it's only sometimes, like once out of every five or six mondays, and usually she'll just bring sandwiches for dinner, or one time she had a coupon and we went to boston market and she got a roasted chicken and we shared it, sitting with the van's door pulled open wide so we could face outside and not get grease all over the seats.

and then the rest of them go to the bible study at the big huge church that's just across the street from school, and i went with them when i was younger, but i complained enough that now she lets me go to the library instead, because i read the bible through three times already and i wanted to try read-ing other books, like books made for adults, because i'd already gone through the children's section too and there were some great stories there, like meg and charles wallace and that book about a girl who was too tall, but for the adult books i had no idea what i really wanted yet, and so i needed time unsupervised to wander through the shelves and pick things out at random and read a few pages and then check them out and stuff them down under my school books where mom wouldn't know they were hiding.

immoral books were all off limits, like the time i borrowed the fifth harry potter book (i hadn't read the other four) from the neighbours who had moved here from australia, and when my mother saw it it was confiscated and taken back to where it belonged, because there won't be any witchcraft in this house.

she took away the harry potter because it was a "known entity", a book her friends had talked about as one to keep an eye out for, but with the other books sometimes you could get lucky when she'd scan them through and not see certain things, but even so it just was easier to hide things if there might be any doubt, like that one time i did the summer reading competition and then won that book by garth nix, sabriel, and had to hide it underneath my mattress because it had parts in it with boys and sex, and it stayed there under the mattress for so long that tiny pebbles wore holes through the cover and through several pages from the mattress shifting slightly every time i crawled onto it when it was time for bed.

underneath the mattress there were other books as well, things i'd gotten for free or a quarter and then whatever latest had come from the library, like the first adult book i got, the one that ended up having weird scenes about someone freezing to death in the cargo hold of a passenger plane and a guy who cut his stomach open to see what his liver looked like, or the book about the two brothers who took acid and screamed about ducks, and then got older and one got super rich and super fat and was paralysed and made girls do gross things just because he could.

my mother dropped me off at the library because i had complained to her repeatedly for an entire year that i wasn't learning anything new at those bible studies because i'd read through the bible more times than the group leaders had etc etc, but the real reason was that those leaders terrified me, with the sort of weird, aggressive look in all their eyes, and then the tracts they'd hand out once each year, about how you had to be scared unless you had accepted jesus properly and really believed, and i believed as hard as i could, believed believed, but still i felt scared and once, when they said they would take you aside if you felt like you needed to, i raised my hand and told this all to one of those ladies, but she didn't have any answers and i just felt scared and scared and knew that i believed, but there was never an answering feeling like they said there would be, of feeling warm and part of something else.

she dropped me at the library because that was the only place that would stay open late enough, and she couldn't take me home because then dad would see and know i hadn't gone to the bible study with everyone else, and that was not an option, so on every monday i would have 4 hours sitting there until the library closed, and it would be almost completely empty, and all dark outside, and i would wander through the shelves and pick out books at random and read one page in and then would put it back unless it made me interested, or else sometimes i'd sit in the "teen section", even though i was just barely now a teen, and read through manga and would draw my own characters using them as references, because i'd gotten interested in manga after that one study period where the greek exchange girl, margaret, had lent me the first volume of one of her shoujo serieses, and there was a girl riding on a bike and talking with boys and making them bentou lunches, and it felt like this was how a real life ought to have been.

November 12th. My Book Report, by Heather Brown.

In this book Shiloh by Phyllis Reynolds Naylor, there is a dog named Shiloh and a boy named Marty who really likes Shiloh a lot and tries to keep him safe.

Dogs are better than other animals, such as cats, because I can lay my head on them and they do not make me sneeze. They are also a lot better because Marty has a dog and I want to be like Marty because he is a cool person, and that is why I like this book. I am a lot like Marty because I also have a dog named Will, and he is very nice and we saved him when he was not treated very nicely by other people. Marty does not like it when Shiloh is hurt, and he tries to keep Shiloh from being hurt by keeping him a secret from his family.

In the book, Marty's dog Shiloh is a beagle, which is small and has short hair. Will is a larger dog and has longer hair, and longer hair is better because it is good for hugs. Will does dog hugs differently from other dogs though because he does not use his tongue to lick people in the face, which is what most dogs do, and instead he licks my legs a lot and it tickles.

My father is weird to Will because when he was younger

he had a different dog and that different dog was like Will except that he was faster and younger and liked to play more games. My father tries to treat Will like that other dog that he had had, but Will cannot do the things that the other dog used to do, and it makes my father sad and he also gets kind of frustrated. This makes me wonder why do people get dogs, because dogs do not live as long as humans, and they only live dog years. So I think this book is also sad, because even though Marty likes Shiloh, Marty will get older and Shiloh will be gone. When Marty gets older, he will probably get another dog and then he will be sad like my father.

in our neighbourhood we have these things called "washes". i used to think that everybody had them, until i had to describe them to somebody who didn't know the word. a wash is a sort of pathway, wide and low, usually made from concrete and with walls to either side. they feel a little like tunnels, tucked away behind the houses, and the trees that hang over the walls make it feel more "closed" and private, like a space outside the world. some washes are big, around 12 feet from bottom, up curved sides, and to the top of the wall, and wide and flat enough to drive a car through i think. some of them are smaller, and they feel like they fit you perfectly, single-human-sized.

the washes are meant to prevent flash flooding, which we get a lot here in the desert. it's because how, in the desert, the ground is hard and flat because there isn't often rain or moisture in the atmosphere. the dirt is always dry, and so the little bits of dirt get all packed down so that it's hard for water, when it comes, to soak down in between them, and it sits on top and flows along and turns into a flood.

the washes run all through the neighbourhood, a little like

a net. or maybe more like veins, the way they join up into bigger washes where all of the water is collected, really big ones where mesquite and cacti grow and that have lots of grass that grows and dies, all super green for days after it rains and then, in a week or two, it disappears and all goes back to brown.

exploring, they can feel like secret passages, that feeling of "behind the scenes", when you cut past peoples' houses and hear them in their backyards and talking and playing and cooking and living their lives, it's like there are all these hundreds of worlds and you could step out at any time to see them, like that bit in narnia about the pools, all this space just opens up for you, and the feeling of it is that, more than even exploring and finding new places and things, it's something about the space itself just being there, like in that same book, earlier there's a scene where the kids find a secret passage in the attic where all the houses are connected, and you can walk along all carefully, keep your feet on the boards where they won't fall through, and it's like you're really *going* somewhere. and then look forwards and there's this sense, when a path stretches on and on way out in front of you that way, there's the feeling that you're going, and you don't know if time is still flowing, and you just walk.

04

the lightning tree

wicked scar all down one side

that field behind the church, and you're remembering how
wild it used to seem. how you'd sneak out there when every-
body was in sunday school, and then you'd climb the lightning
tree, the biggest tree you've ever seen, and just the reaching
that first fork is hard enough, takes a running jump and up the
side and grabbing on a smaller branch and swinging yourself
over, to the knook that you've worn smooth, smooth and cool
beneath your feet, something living that won't leave you when
you need it to be there

you climb the tree to read. and you read to pass the time. and
you pass the time until the service ends, and then you drop
down noiselessly and join the string of children leaving class
together, join the group, looking for parents, you are hidden
in the crowd

05

i like to be in high places.

i like to look down on the world, so that everything looks really small and i can see the way it all fits together.

and i can climb any tree. if you can point to it, i can climb it. even the trees with thorns or the trees that have no branches until twenty feet in the air.

i used to read a series of books called The Boxcar Children, and in one of those books there is a boy who grew up on a desert island, all on his own. his feet are hard and callused, just like mine, and that's where i learned the trick of how to climb any tree. the trick is to support yourself with your feet, keeping them underneath you with the soles pressed to the bark so your knees stick out to either side at sharp angles. you push your feet down and lift yourself up, like an accordion lift, and then you grab and hold yourself up with your arms while you pull your feet in again.

it also works with things like ropes or poles. in fact, it's a lot easier with metal poles because they're smooth, so your feet can lay flat against them and can get a better grip. that's because of friction, which means that, the more of a thing is touching, the more they "stick together" when you try to slide them along each other. our skin is really good at friction because of the oils, and also the way we have patterns on our hands and feet, though how that part works i'm not really sure about.

sometimes, when nobody's watching, i climb lamp posts all the way up and hang by my hands from the thin bars at the top. it feels really dangerous up there, like i'm going to fall, or like the whole lamp post is going to fall under me, and if i fell from there i would definitely die because it's so high up. i also get really scared that i'm getting heavier and will make the things fall over because i weigh too much, even though i'm still only 70 pounds, which is a lot lighter than everyone else. i get really scared, but i still do it, because climbing is what i'm best at, and so if i'm not best at that then i'm not at anything.

one time i was going to a competition in a building, and walking up to it i suddenly had that urge to climb, so i took off my shoes and started up a lamp post, but a lady from inside saw me and came running out in heels and shouted at me, so i only got halfway up. i don't understand heels. my mom tried to make me wear them once, but they just hurt my feet and i couldn't even run, so i'm never going to wear them again.

the thing that's the most fun to climb is the swingset at the park, and that's because it's the hardest. because first you have to hold yourself up with just your arms while you get all the sand off your feet, because otherwise your feet won't be able to grip the pole. then the whole way up you have to work really hard to keep yourself from spinning around sideways, because the pole is at an angle so it's easy to end up hanging underneath it instead of being on top, and if you're hanging underneath you can't pull yourself up over the top bar.

once i'm all the way up there, i like to watch all the kids down below running around. there's this game we all play sometimes where four people get on all four of the swings and then swing back and forth. then someone else has to run between the bars all the way to the other side, dodging the people swinging. sometimes another person will throw things like nerf footballs at the person running that they have to dodge.

the other ones that i like better are the super simple jumping one, where you see who can jump the furthest and mark it with a line in the sand where your feet landed (or your bottom, if you fall over backwards) and then the shoe-tossing game. in the shoe-tossing one, you have to swing and then fling your shoes and aim for targets. there are these three round cylinder things across the sand that all have open tops, and you have to get the shoe into the cylinders. the yellow one is worth the most because it's the tallest, so it's harder to get them in.

mostly, though, i just climb up and watch while other people play. it's a lot easier to see everything that's going on from up there, so i act as the referee and can see a lot of things that other people can't. i do really wish someone would come up there and sit with me, though. nobody else likes to climb, so whenever i do it i'm always alone.

06

The Urban Heat Island effect is a proposed mechanism by which urban areas can become and remain significantly warmer than their surroundings, most notably so at night. It is thought to be the result of coating surfaces with man-made materials, such as concrete and asphalt, which absorb solar radiation readily and from which heat is not so quick to be evaporated away as in more vegetated areas. Other significant factors are thought to be tall buildings, which can impede cooling winds, and pollutants, which contribute to a greenhouse effect. As a city grows, the increase in surface area works to compound these effects.

– Dr. E.H. Vandiskew

"Why, you don't know the half of it!", says old Ltoiotl emphatically. "When I was a pup, I remember it used to get so cold at night that the whole city would freeze right over. All the cars and planes, and even the river, would just freeze right in place and have to wait there until they could move again after the morning thaw. Every night our mothers would make us hot potato stew, and we'd pack it under our coats to keep ourselves warm while we played. I remember one night when Chliili's mother had made him only half a batch (because they were poor, you know), and then his right arm and leg both froze completely solid, and we had to help him to limp all the way home.

We used to take the little frozen birds down from their perches and then place them somewhere else, on towers and fence-posts and windowsills, and in the morning when they thawed the poor little things would be so confused. 'Did I really fall asleep *there*?'. It was childish perhaps, but we needed a way to pass the time, since time itself would start to freeze and move more slowly on those nights.

At first you might think it's only you were only feeling a little sluggish, and that maybe the reason it took a little longer to tie your shoes was because your hands were starting to go numb. Then you would notice that the moon looked to be still fixed in place where you had seen it earlier, and that even the clouds were drifting past so slowly now you'd need a time-lapse camera to catch them in the act. And during the very coldest depths of the very harshest winter nights you might have an entire month pass by before the moon would set and sun came back to warm things up again.

How could we measure a month had gone by if the sun and the moon weren't moving? Well, just trust me.

There were games we played back then, on those longest of nights. Games that elsewhere would have been dominated by quick reflexes and feats of physical prowess, in our world they became all cleverness and tactics. Footballs kicked and snowballs thrown, you can see how it becomes a sort of puzzle, weaving through a wave of slowly-moving spheres, pulling off the perfect dodge and planning out the next attack. More strategic by half than either shougi or chess, and with our brains kept warm by thinking so furiously that we experienced every moment of positioning and stop-frame dodge-and-weave. It was a perfect preparation for the stressful world to come.

And then sometimes during those nights, though maybe not I think now so often as we really ought to have done, but there were sometimes we would call out to our mothers and ask them to come and join us there, come and join us in the snow and to see the frozen moths, so delicate and hanging lightly in the air, or once a single painted hummingbird gone lost from his migration, and his wingbeats slown to just a beat per minute, come and look, come and see! They always declined us, though. 'Our place is inside', they said, 'and we will be here, waiting for you to return'. And so we would come back to them, to the smell of buttered pancakes ready laid out for breakfast, and to the knowledge that we were home.

Miss those nights? Of course we do. Time passes so much more quickly these days, now that we are grown."

some places are cold

some places have snow

once upon a time your father took you to a very cold place, and you told yourself: "i can deal with this". you wore only the thinnest sweater, left the front unzipped, and it was 15 fahrenheit, and you were trying to be brave

your father bought himself a thing of shrimp with dipping sauce, and he sat and ate his way through half the tray, the sort that's meant for parties, circular and large, for when a mother's not prepared and has to rush to get something be-cause the father says "my friends are coming over" and it's 4-o-clock already, and it works out in the end because the shrimp and other platters really are enough when everyone is drunk by half an hour in, a flood of margaritas and of beer, and the daughter of a somebody is sitting next to you, there on the swing, and you try your very best to get along, show her you're cool and that you understand how parents work and school and all of that, and you are 15 and are drunk, and so is she, and words are sort of difficult, and it surprises you when suddenly you're both behind the shed and she's on top of you and doing certain things with mouth and hands, and you are feeling sort of slow and left behind but struggle to catch up again, and rocks are poking in your back, and part of you is worrying that there are scorpions, and you are very drunk, and margarita burns your stomach and your chest, and then it really doesn't matter any more because the now becomes a gone, because the rough becomes a soft and is a warm

.   .   .

they find you there, next morning, and it doesn't go so well. the finding part and then the 3 years following besides

.   .   .

your father makes it halfway through the platter, sitting in an empty park, at a table, underneath a tree that hasn't any leaves, and he sits there for a while and you think that he is thinking, and you wonder what it is that fathers think about, in bed at night, their breathing going ragged and then turning into snore, and you think it must be something very powerful, to keep them down in spite of all the noise o8

"well. so this is where you get out"

your father says, and paddles the car to the side of the road

he does not want you here. you are unwanted

tried to leave you with an uncle, but you ran away from there,
and he was forced to take you back but it was only for a while,
and now the deal was that you turn 18 and that's the end of
it, figure things out, your life, not mine

do what you want, but somewhere i don't have to watch

but you can't let it go so easily; there's too much been unsaid,
and so you chase and make him stop the car, try to pull yourself
inside and ask him please please, please tell me what you want,
tell me what can i do, anything

pries your fingers from his seatbelt, one-by-one, closes the door
and drives away and leaves you drowning on the curb

09

walking home one day, and you are reading while you walk. the story of a girl who is a monster. who is her mother.

walking home, and cutting through the wash, and it is one hundred and seven degrees fahrenheit and you are feeling cold. you pull a sweatshirt from your bag (you keep it there because the bus and buildings all are freezing) and you swap the book from hand to hand and pull the sweatshirt over arms and zip it to your neck, and there your fingers brush against your neck, the feel of something crawling, and now suddenly you're terrified; this book is eating you

. . .

walking home one day, and you are reading while you walk. as you're cutting through the wash, you nearly step in something that is red and brown and white and dead. rabbits in the neighbourhood, and this one's upper torso has gone wandering and left the rest behind to dry: "same gotta eat. birds and worms."

coyote came and went. the pawprints in the dirt are only visi-
ble because the ground is softened here. the wash after a rain

oa

aug 10

it's so difficult to find people to hang out with, because every-
one else my age went to college while i'm spending all day at
work. and every day is hectic and stressful but it's also just
so boring, especially at the grocery store, everyone else who
works there is twenty or thirty years older than me, and they
have these fixed routines like work to bar to work again like
they're scared of someone reminding them they're still alive
and doing everything they can to forget about it, and always
smoking on every break. that scares me...

at the library is a little better, because there i can wear
headphones and people mostly don't bother me except for
asking questions sometimes, or there's always someone who's
drunk or high or whatever, but that isn't so bad, and head-
phones mean this way i can listen to books all day and then
read on the way home afterwards, which i know some people
would say is just the same as pretending not to be alive, try
to escape reality, but it doesn't feel that way, or else if this is
an escape then maybe i'd rather have books and reading than

33

a "real world life" anyways, because it's the only way to experience more than just these things immediately in front of us and learn and think about life in different worlds. people weren't made to live like this, going home to work to home every day and never anything that changes . . . . or maybe they were, but then once you've poisoned yourself with a little bit of reading and what it's like to see the world then maybe it isn't possible afterwards, to go back

.   .   .

aug 14

every day on the path walking home i pass through two different worlds

maybe that's being overly-dramatic, but it really feels that way. over by main street are all these fancy, big apartments made for rich people, and everything is clean and trimmed and grassy lawns for interstitial parks that have "no pooping" signs for dogs, and little benches where people can come from the corner ice-cream shop and sit and talk together, butterscotch ripple, i wonder if that's a real flavour, snozzberries

so first pass through this strip of wealth and gang of prison workers cleaning, and then cross the street and all of it falls away, replaced with used-car lots and all-packed-together the strip clubs and loan centres and other things people don't want to see. concrete and trash and empty dirt, and little houses falling down, and mexican restaurants scattered here and there. it's a half-joking joke i'll tell people who come from out of town, "it's not an authentic mexican restaurant if there are no bullet holes in the walls", but kind of true, look for the place that's proud of plastic tables and chairs and paper plates, or sometimes foil, and drink dispenser in the corner has to have manzana soda, and the green and red sauces are in unlabelled squeeze bottles, and home-made tortillas so strong and thin they turn translucent in the light, and concrete or tiling on the floor and windows heavy-metal barred

ah but really i don't really meet many people from out of town these days, so this is mostly just a dialogue in my head

•   •   •

sep 17

i mostly listen to fiction books, but have also now started to add some nonfiction things, because if i'm not going to college then maybe this can be like a replacement education. todays was chinese history, how to tell apart the ming and qing and xia, and all those northern tribes and mongols and then becoming manchu, and splitting and merging and being Chosen Under Heaven. it's strange how well it all coheres into "a history", though maybe part of that's revisionist (in a bad way) and it really was more like the scattered tribes of celtic languages, how ideas float here and there and back and forth between people but it's not like there's some higher level authority that ties them all together

anyways i like history best because it's like something real but also far away

actually, speaking of college though, i've also started heading over to campus and sneaking into some of the bigger lectures there. it's easy with those bigger classes because they fill up entire auditoriums full of people, and i look the right age so nobody ever asks. i got tuesday-thursdays off at work and that way have been going to some classes every week, world history and PSYCH 101, which is also interesting but i'm not too sure how seriously to take it, because there's all that talking recently about a "reproducibility crisis" where certain experiments didn't work when other people tried them, and the professor talked about this one experiment on what's called priming, where they gave people hot coffee and it made them more "warm and friendly", but that was one of the things i heard that couldn't be repeated and he didn't mention there was any doubt about it. it makes me wonder, how much is it ok to trust people, or if everything for everyone is just pieced together from personal annecdotes and biases

and what is trust anyways? and knowing people. sometimes it can feel like i'm trapped here inside my head, and all of these books are just other voices in here, talking to me but like they don't really exist anywhere else, out in the world

ob

"...yes?"

telephone at 21 when you're already sleeping. a number you
don't recognise; the voice is strange as well

she says "ah uhm, oh wait, ah whoops, i'm sorry, i mis-dialed",
and she moves to go but stops and asks a question

"hey, do you know anything about carpentry?"

she works at a haunted house downtown, is walking there right
now, got to prepare things for october, lots of set building to
do

footsteps and cars

a plane?

back and forth exchanging movies, sorry, horror is no good, no,
i get it, and that's why i work here actually, a sort of variolation,
forced-exposure-makes-you-well. a risky business though

she says it's her favourite: *la science des rêves*, and you watch it
while you talk with her, this too-cute boy from mexico moves
to a paper town, and you're feeling very sleepy and you lis-
ten to her voice, sort of gruff and rumble grumble, rough and
pleasant against your jaw, hold the phone there feel it vibrat-
ing, the noises of her work, hammer saw, she's assembling the
backing of a scene, and you float in semi-consciousness and
wait until she's done

•　　•　　•

sueño en otro idioma, bits of spanish, japanese

catches you off guard, when a setting is trilingual and you only
know the two, english, french, and spanish; english, japanese,
and mandarin; skip the rails on foreign phrases and your brain
stops in its tracks, "what is real?"

every morning you wake up disoriented being human, single
person in a body in a single place in time, how does this make
any sense, what is sense, "karl popper", "willard quine"

"why am i inside a monkey?"

it takes you several minutes and anxiety returns, that familiar
dread of being anything

. . .

something in french movies you can't catch, and it's not just
the language barrier, though that's a part as well, but the way
the world is large-but-small and sort of mismatched colours,
doesn't care about your feelings, ugly patterns, crumble walls

not simple like the houses here that everyone aspires to, show
you're rich by throwing things away

you talk with her for hours but forget to ask her name, and
when the morning comes and she walks home again she's still
there talking, says ah shit, my battery is dying, runs to get a
cable, and you hear her trip and think the phone gets dropped
into the pool

never hear from her again

oct 19

i'm feeling sort of... disconnected maybe. holding onto an identity, it gets difficult when you're living behind the scenes and always watching. reality and fiction and your life can all get blurred together, and there isn't any coherent theme to build it all around. *records of a floating life*, like that, a part of it could go away missing and no one would be able to tell, all disjunctive fragmentation. maybe that's how real life actually works, though, our experiences. in the intro literature class i stopped by to the other day that's what the professor said, that "women's writing is characterised by disjunctive fragmentation and a focus on familial relations", or however it was he put it, and since i haven't got the family side then maybe that's just normal, that it all just comes apart and floats away

speaking of that shen fu though, maybe i should try gardening. i don't have enough money to support a pet or anything, but growing plants, keeping something in a planter by a window at least could work, and pair it with a little zero-maintenance stone garden or so. always thought it was so interesting, those bonsai, these plants and scenes in miniature, and things that usually grow like a bush or woody vines, when you trim them down that way it's like you can see what they'd be like as real trees, tall and twisted-tangled, knotted branches, giant roots, these little places that look so perfect but you can't ever visit them, stuck in your giant outsider's body looking in

•   •   •

oct 21

maybe keeping a garden is too optimistic

roommate wanted to make tacos, so we borrowed this electric griddle from the neighbours, and that was kind of fun, but then she accidentally left it on all night and it burnt out, and so now we'll have to buy a new one and that probably means no more food this week. or maybe i can find one of those student events where they're always giving away free pizza

my roommmate esther, she isn't a bad person i don't think, just a little spacey, doing an art degree and brings home to work on her projects sometimes, or carrying around her sketchbook and drawing sketches of random things in the house or sometimes people, on the times that we'll go out together for groceries, because it's easier going to walk toghether with

someone when you're carrying bags like that, the mile from
the store back to home, together it doesn't feel so far, even if
we never talk. but sometimes she'll just stop and set down
her bags and then start sketching someone, and then i'll wait
there watching her and how these shapes come into being sort
of hazily, big patches and shadows and then more detailing,
a lot like carving things from marble, or at least how that gets
described

she did a sketch of me too once, as a portrait, felt so strange,
instead of only always watching, like a proof that other people
are watching too and that i'm something they can see

she filled in such big dark circles under my eyes, and i
looked in the mirror afterwards and was surprised, seeing they
were really there

· · ·

nov 2

today i stayed on campus until after it got dark. it's like a dif-
ferent place at night, without the people everywhere rushing
to classes in a flood, and the sun is gone and sprinklers on and
there's moisture in the air, and all these open, open spaces,
makes you really want to run, took off my shoes and put down

my bag and just started running across the soccer field and then suddenly it was muddy and my feet were kind of splattered so i found one of the sprinklers and sat back on my hands and stuck my feet in front to wash them off, sprinklers back and forth, and looking up at the sky so flat like a ceiling here made me think about hitchhiker's guide, krikkit, never looking up, and are we like that here in citites maybe, living in a little diorama and cut off from that perspective of there being something like a "universe", only people, rushing here and rushing there, but maybe sun and moon at least can be enough of a reminder, systems aren't ever closed

it feels like this could get addicting, staying out alone at night. have to be careful though; the last train runs at 1 am od

campus exploring, like a maze

the doors have all got locks, but there are ways to get around
them, push with force just right and the latch comes free, or
slide something between, or as a last resort just wait till some-
one passes and then tag along behind

up the stairwell, through the hall, a bridge with full-height
windows

hand-made posters on the walls to hand-made advertise, and
people scribble on their neighbours' doors to share anony-
mously, say i hate you, think you're perfect, jeez quit whining,
i'm not your mom, and next time try to clean the oven when
you use it, like a bomb went off in there

hello, my name is:

people sometimes leave doors open, let you walk inside and
join a little party, awkward children in a circle, plastic cups
and wooden faces, moving sluggishly, a mix of malnutrition,

last night's hangover, the dregs of puberty

one girl is always there, sitting cross-legged in the hallway, and the third or fourth time that you see her she calls out to you, and so you sit down next to her, can barely see her grassy eyes, golden hair down to the floor that waves and curls and makes you want to brush or braid or anything, just an excuse to feel it smooth against your hands

and you think "uhm"

and just sit there for an hour, neither of you say a thing, until you see the time and stand and rush to catch the midnight train. and you end up coming back to her, one night, two nights, and four, and you sit and don't say anything and stand to leave again

after a while she starts to hold your hand

you cannot be the thing she needs, but there's still worth in trying

you stay with her because she's drunk and high and half to crying and you want to be her eyes oe

nov 11

javelina come down from the mountain, running in bands. they eat up peoples' gardens and spread garbage everywhere. they make me feel actually afraid

"gregarious". there's a lot of speculation goes into that, ideas like "human communal living was instrumental in developing a superior intellect". social hierarchies and bearing fangs, projecting signals, javelina clatter their teeth, and how it's always better to simulate a fight than risk the damages for real. that all seems too "guy-oriented", though

or maybe i'm just sexist. or just weird, being alone

that's one thing makes me admire coyote, though. with javelina or wolves you always see them in a group, always relying on each other and those ties, but coyote lives more flexibly, can wander here and there and forage independently and then at night sometimes they'll start to sing and all meet up again to join a hunt

it's that flexibility that's let them respond so successfully to humans, while the wolves have ended up nearly extinct. they can eat anything, they can live anwhere. when angry farmers hunt them they'll respond by having larger broods, 400 thousand years of being hunted by wolf neighbours, population regulation, limits to growth

they can interbreed with dogs and wolves but still make up a species of their own. that sort of seamless transition between the worlds, i want that

• • •

nov 12

been thinking a lot more about animals since yesterday. maybe i'll start a separate journal or something

earlier saw a roadrunner. the sort of thing would be too frightening if it was somehow to grow larger, terror birds. i guess the mammals have monopoly on that size range by now, though. like how giant insects only lasted up until the vertebrates moved in, and meganeuridae longer than most because the first pterosaurs had not yet started flying and displaced them from the air

the roadrunner, it has these eyes with pupils used for spying, chasing prey. this tiny therapod has a big fat lizard by the throat and, with those jerking motions only low-mass animals

can manage, it will pull it back and bash it against a rock, over
and over, looking for any twitching sign of life

    rushing, stabbing, beating, biting, balancing tails that help
them jump and run. extensible mohawk headcrests, and can't
tell the sexes apart, no outwardly visible dimorphism, so their
cruelty is shared

    preying on scorpions despite the neurotoxins, how do they
live

    scorpions.... what's it called, some kind of tropism. like
bats, how they tend to hang upside-down, bark scorpions in-
stinctively crawl and hang, avoid the ground, you'll find them
on the walls and ceilings, watch your feet and watch your
head, or somewhere dark under your blanket, in the pantry,
hiding in bags or boxes of food, you go to pour something and
out comes a scorpion plop into the bowl

    crawling on a piece of paper, hear their tiny scritchey feet

    i average maybe one sting a year, or probably a little higher.
on a limb the pain will sort of travel up in waves up towards
the body's core, and if it catches you on a finger the venom can
make it go numb for days. one crawled up my back once and
down my top, stung twice in the chest, it made my heart start
fibrillating, really freaked out

    wonder, if the body ever builds immunity, or if i've just got-
ten more used to the pain. at least have got slightly more body-

mass now than when i was younger. i was first stung when very small, around 40 to 50 pounds, while i was out playing in the backyard at night. running back and forth and one of them caught me on the bottom of the foot, so sort of half-run hopped inside to a couch, and just remember breathing very shallowly and body moving on its own, and the couch had one of those throws that people call a "mexican blanket", a sarape, gradient lines and a diamond pattern in brown, white, and blue, and vague awareness of family all there with me, fussing around and wipe-your-forehead, hush now everything's fine

we used to stop and shout to call someone whenever a scorpion was seen, "get a shoe!", but by now i've worked out how to handle them efficiently. just always keep a broom and some duct tape around, a sticky bit rolled up at the very end of the handle. scorpions run on a sort of simplistic program, these little automata, so if you act predictably then they always will too. move in slowly with the broom handle, more quickly and they run, but slowly and they just sit there waiting and try and sting when it gets close, so you can catch them stuck on the tape without any worry they'll get away

arthropoda from the ocean, they have these underside gills adapted for the air, call them book lungs, with flaps like pages, one of those size limiters that keep them in their niche. though sea scorpions could get up past two metres apparently, those millions of years ago

i've gotten pretty used to being stung, but the fear of it is still there. and that first moment after, when you feel that tiny jab but the real pain still hasn't started yet, and there's nobody around and you know what's about to happen, need to deal with it on your own...

· · ·

dec 16

esther wanted to have a christmas party, some of her friends from school aren't going home this year, so everyone's coming over tonight to celebrate with them. i'm a little nervous about that, all these people i don't know, but she says it's fine because they're mostly art kids and won't do anything crazy, just smoke a little and we should make some hummus, and she got this film, *sleep dealer*, everyone can watch

of

circle on the floor and people rocking back and forth, can al-
most feel it second-handed, deprivation, lights are dimmed,
motions all exaggerated, feel the swaying of the world

this little house is all filled-up, a pregnancy, both senses of the
word

decided against smoking; all the people here are strange; want
to meet them, if you meet them, while awake

the finger-foods are gone but there is still a spread of beer,
standing in the corner kitchen, icy tile under your toes, crouch
in front of the refrigerator, tiny little thing, and tuck two beers
into the ice tray, jealous squirrel

a leg appears, long toes and turned-up jeans. "so you're the
roommate, was it?"

.   .   .

exchanging names

exchanging-games

play the game of information, dance between the lines, with
this boy who smells of sandalwood and listens to what you say,
really hearing and responding like nobody ever does

makes you feel an idiot, stare the corner of his mouth, little
curling-up in smiling is like "i know who you are", and you've
never felt so naked, look away

you are as red as a very red thing

information, he takes you for all you're worth and then gives
nothing in return. 俺の勝ち, 完全な失敗 it is

I O

dec I7

he asked me out for curry, and i said yes.

so i guess that's tomorrow. his family lives here too, so he doesn't have to leave for christmas stuff. or maybe they don't celebrate it, but that's probably too forwards to ask about, ah i don't know. i can't think clearly at all; everything's all fuzzy and weird and is it ok to get excited about something like this? or maybe it's too late to ask that, but still, it's also kind of scary, like i've never done this kind of thing before and don't know what to expect and what if it ends up a disappointment then i'll have built it into this whole big thing in my head and then will definitely be awkward around him if we see each other again later, which he's esther's friend so of course i'll see him...

and it was already so awkward when he asked me where we should go, like i instinctively said "curry" and it was basi-cally like saying "yes, i am a clueless sheltered girl and that is the extent of what i associate with india, food, and you make me think of food", and so then add the caveat "thai curry" and that totally made it worse but he just brushes over it but i bet he was really thinking that i'm so stupid

aaaa wanna die XX

and then what even is there to wear...

· · ·

dec 19

did not go as expected, what am i even supposed to be feeling. so we went to the thai place and i got "the red one" and he got "green", and so that was fine except i was really nervous and awkard and so ate too quickly without saying anything and then was sitting there finished while he still had more left. but he's really good at talking so it turned out ok, and i actually found out a few things about him like his grandmother, she never learnt english and so he tries to use his broken telegu to talk with her but is embarrassed about not being able to keep up and respond, which made me a lot less nervous just hearing, that there's something he feels awkward about too

(or at least i *think* it was telegu he said, but there are so many languages around there, right? XX)

so that turned out ok, and then instead of taking me home he drove over to his parents house but didn't tell them we were there and instead went around the back and brought back this tandem bicycle that they've had forever and apparently his parents used to ride as a joke, and he got me to try it with him, which wasn't as hard as i thought it would have been though i wasn't the one steering, and the night was all dark and cold and we got going really fast, probably too fast, and were doing fine up until we got to the park turned onto the grass and then slipped because it was all wet, and my jeans got torn up on the calf and it was kind of bleeding... but it was actually really fun and didn't hurt at all, like maybe it was the extra shot of adrenaline falling over but we both just started laughing and couldn't stop, and then i started running and tried to do a cartwheel like an idiot and fell in a big puddle and was all covered in the recycled poopwater they use for irrigation, which was pretty gross and embarrassing (or i guess it's probably actually greywater and they have to actually treat it first so it's not all full of whatever dangerous bacteria, but still it smelled kind of bad...)

so then we snuck into his parents place through the back door and tried to stay all quiet to not wake them up while i tried to wash myself off some and borrowed a pair of shorts, and then he came in the bathroom with me after (once i had clothes back on!) and had a first-aid kit and wrapped up my leg, which that was surprising because i'd washed it off but then completely forgot about it, and he was so careful, the way he was holding my leg in place with one hand and putting on disinfectant with the other, and then he wrapped the bandage around all slowly and deliberately while i'm sitting on the edge of the tub and looking down at the top of his head that's all curly and black and it felt... i don't know, i've never felt that before, kind of hot and heart going crazy but also at the same time calm, and like almost scared to move or say anything like it will ruin the moment

i just want to see him again

. . .

jan 11

got really distracted this past few weeks. didn't see him again because he was doing family stuff, and then esther too went off with her family, so i was here alone reading the whole time and doing other things trying not to think too much; found out a bunch of universities post lectures online for free, especially MIT has their open coursware stuff, but also just searching youtube etc there are professors from all over who've posted all their lectures probably for students to follow along, so if you know the right things to search for a lot of stuff is there, especially maths and computer stuff. Also podcasts are amazing, there are a bunch of scientists who go on places to talk about their research but also do their own entire shows and go over bigger topics, or do reviews of interesting new papers when they come out. it's really fun and feels like i've learned so much so quickly (though that's probably an illusion, probably forgotten most of it already)

but so then esther came back because her classes started up on monday. and then yesterday i met up with him again in the afternoon and we stopped by his research lab where they do robotics stuff i guess, and i came in and hung around in a corner while people worked

it was a little awkward, all these mostly guys, there was one girl who came by for a moment but she left again quickly, and they were all talking about cryptocoins, or i heard this one guy telling someone all proudly about how he was working with one of those companies that does digital coursework and collects all gradeschooler's data, their test scores and essays and everything, and keeps everything and then offers it to universities afterwards so they "know what to expect" or something, that's honestly too creepy and makes me glad my school was way behind on tech stuff and had no computers and did everything by hand

it was better after that, though. after he finished working on things we left and then stopped by the apartment of this

really nice grad school couple living together near campus,
and we all smoked and then sat around talking until really
late when i went to catch the train

II

leave his lab and walk together, heading back to home, and cut

across the campus, quicker-way, and stop

on this dormitory's front lawn are bubble blowers, and some-

one has filled the decorative fountain up with soap, and it is

bubbling and whitened froth in mountains and their hills

spill over in abundance and are covering the lawn

students fighting, play, chase down and plaster one another in

a shimmer outer-coating carapace

enthusia, your body feeling light

moments that break from their surroundings, continuity gone

frozen in my mind, thought-forms enshrined

ものの脆み、刹那的、mono no awareness-of-soon-coming-to-

an-end, things that break-before-they-bend, so this single spot

in time, try to suspend

and which of these is best: the life that runs itself in loops, the life that stretches on away, the life that vanishes into a puff of smoke

whichever one is true, and all are true... it hurts to think of it

wonder at these membranes, irredescent, and how far can they be stretched, how thin they are, the arrangement of lipids into a molecular monolayer made macroscopic, there between water and air, jittering tails out in the wind, he dances with the bubble-blower, teasing out, so delicate, dark night and halogen overhead shines through contrasting, shut your eyes and still you see, images return to me, 永遠に

.   .   .

an aggressive sort of happiness, so hard and fast and makes you feel afraid

1 2

feb 18

so, , , he and esther are already dating, i guess. esther goes out a lot, and i didn't think about that at all before because we both do our own stuff and we don't want to bother each other. only this time i heard someone drove here to pick her up, and so i got kind of curious and looked out the window and there he is with her, and they're all talking casually and she gave him one of those like fake-angry play shoves and then they both got in his car and kissed before he drove away

i don't know what was i expecting, like i kept thinking "you'd better not get your hopes up and get too invested", because nothing's ever worked out before, but then i did anyways and now of course something like this happens, and actually i guess they must have been going out since before we even met before that party, and probably they did stuff together over christmas break while i was there all fussing around worrying about being awkward seeing him again, which is kind of...

well, but then he still hasn't mentioned anything about it even though we've already... yeah, so i guess maybe he was never going to? or maybe she knows already and this is just a normal thing for them or something

well then either it's one or the other. but like either way i don't really want to say anything about it, because either it's fine and i'm intruding or else it's not fine and then everything turns into a big mess, and with esther too...

. . .

mar 17

his apartment is kind of a mess. but i guess that's just typical boys' stuff. there's a big open-top trashcan that's always overflowing, like no one ever takes it out

we make dinner and watch movies sometimes, or people come over and everyone drinks too much, but that's still fun because i get to meet new people every time. this one friend group who all do theatre, i asked them a bunch of questions about acting and like how differently people will interpret the same play or stage directions etc, how much it's ok to improvise. nobody would call "friends" yet, though

oh, and it's not just me and esther either apparently. there was another girl who came over today to see him, and they got all touchy standing around in the kitchen when i was right

there, so i guess that's just how stuff is. maybe he assumes i
knew about him and esther from before? but then it's true that
i actually do know, so it's not like i have anything to complain
about

   slowly starting to get warmer; i wonder if there's anywhere
around here i can swim

·   ·   ·

came home from work just now and almost stepped on a coy-
ote lying on the sidewalk. hit by a car? he was still barely
breathing but didn't look too great, and there was a bunch of
blood, and so i sort of ran thinking "i'll get help" or something
but then realised that was stupid and just went back to the
house and then got here and was crying a bunch and it took
a long time to calm down, and the mailbox is all jammed full
of advertisements and bills for people who don't live here any
more, a roberto and jed and marisa and sean and what does
the person delivering all of these letters think, that we really
have 14 other people all living in this tiny house seven people
to a bed?, and i don't know where to put these like it's a felony
to mess with them, isn't it?, but there's no space left in there

for anything being delivered to me, these people and i'm just
another one all passed around from place to place and having
no real home

follows you. here and there. books back on the shelves. he is following, the man, while you are shelving books, and thinks that you can't see him, or he knows but doesn't care, or maybe knows and he enjoys, likes the way that you are warying, discomfited, and pull your shoulders in, take a book off of the cart and slide it up into its slot but quickly pull away again, the way he sees you from the side, feeling self-conscious, you can hear him start to smile

"nice ass"

is it, so walk away and wait, is what they said to do, until he leaves, let someone know and wait, the sorting room, staff only so it's safe

but corners you, two walls and dark and he makes up the third, because a man who you don't know is something very like a wall, something broad and hard and in your face and you can't move your arms, and it reminds you, of that time when you were staying with a friend and she was keeping pit bulls,

brought back from the shelter, no one wanted, and these crea-
tures they weigh near as much as you and muscles sliding, says
"come on! come play with them", and has you grab onto the
rope and you are thrown around and feeling like your bones
have all dissolved, that sort of muscle and rigidity, the mean-
ing of the word "inexorable", or like you're halfway out and
wading in the ocean, and here come the waves in waves and
you can clear them gracefully, a little hop and carry over and
you're feeling so relaxed until what's this your feet are sliding,
and no air and turned around, your face is grind into the sand
and limbs have somehow gotten lost, feeling salt and tasting
darkness and you wait for it to end and on the beach again
and roll onto your side and start to crawl out of the water, and
your innocence is gone

and when the man is done with you, and fairly quickly, with
how drunk he is and barely gets his hands under your shirt,
he turns away and out the side door of the building, and you
readjust your bra and grab the cart of books half-shelved, back
to the sorting room and don't tell anyone

14

you are shopping out for food, at 13:49 on tuesday, early au-
tumn, and foot traffic fairly light. some children and their
mothers, hustlebustle, sheep-and-dog

wandering the aisles, you pick some cans and carbohydrates.
avoid the meats, you are a vegetarian, decided it was best

or rather that the sight of it can make you want to vomit, makes
you cough and gag and almost start to cry, and you are weak
and are avoiding that whole section of the store and all those
people, eating pieces of themselves, whoa boy, yum yum, love
a pig, love a nice pork roast cut chops over-fire done-right gas-
grill get the seasoning the garlic-lemon-pepper and there's no-
salt-added, worry for your blood pressure no more

no more please. no more

fill it up, fill your brain up, fat gut gristle grastle bone break
marrow dig it out suck slaver brittle porous haemogenesis, drip
drip drip, crush it out, suck suck, beat it down SMACK tender
leave a Big Brown Mark, suck it up, mmm juicy, suck it up

and jittering a bit, and then over to the line, and the lady looks
you over, doesn't speak but makes a face and then turns back
towards the register and poking at the keys, peck peck

.   .   .

outside is very dry and very flat. the temperatures wait un-
til september's at its end before they start to change at all,
feel that dip and it's disorienting, what country is this, a place
where standing on the street won't burn you red and brown
and dead is somewhere new, somewhere alien to you, every
year you're never able to "accustom" to the change, just as
frozen, just as burning, as the day when you were born off in
that hospital that's east a little ways, who knows why that hos-
pital, except that hospitals are things that change with time
as much as anything, and so it's maybe sensical that you were
born in one and siblings all were born in others, and this space
between your pasts, the self-same-space that stands between
you still, the interstice of years

sick to move, sick to think, sick to even breathe

barfed on floor the smell reminds, old dog, he used to do

twinging bile and mucus, smell of grass

all animals us

. . .

you call in work and tell them, hours later when your body starts to function just enough that you can crawl out of the bathroom to the bed

unhappy, disappointed, "irresponsible, you know!"

"we can't have people who behave this way, and so don't bother coming back."

you put the phone aside and gerogero till there's nothing left to come

16

happy are the poor, for theirs is the pleasure of little things

to catch between your hashi
a single grain of rice
and chew it with incisors, carefully

to sew another button
on a well-worn pair of shorts
you found it on the sidewalk, just outside the grocery store

the boy invites you over, and together with his sister you will
play a game of cards, fake bets

from under the table he pulls, a plastic bag that's filled with
coins; nickles, pennies, dimes and quarters, ruffle-jumble rat-
tling

"these useless coins", he laughs, "these useless coins won't buy
you anything that matters, are not worth the being made"

you want to ask him: "can i keep them if i win?"

but it's a breach of etiquette, and you cannot win anyways;
with money games it's he's the one who's shrewd

his laugh turns sour when he sees the colour in your eyes

niggle in his perfect smile

eye-of-the-needle, button-sewn, suck it in and try to fit, here
shariputra, you are emptiness

a seed of hunger-envy starts to grow

17

greasy

is the word, and regret, these sheets

waking up in someone else's room

he's slipped away while you were still asleep apparently, and you've been sliding down the slope towards the centre of the bed, where his body-borne impression is a gulf

sticky-floor, step step, ah, no, someone's there, grab a blanket and you slip across the hall. he looked a little shocked, room-mates; he looked a little small. he turned a little red and he turned his head away and then kept turning off inside himself, an isolated storm, and while you pee you hear him leaving, through the haze of throbbing head, and then the breath comes out of you again, relax

• • •

scrub. scrub scrub

spray, wipe, turn-around, spray, scrub scrub, scrub away,
all the mess-of-many-months, cheese-crisp, processed-sausage,
bits-of-bacon, plastic-package bargain-bin, and it was crack,
hiss, sputter, and a spray became a film and now it's you here
now, scrub-a-scrub, scrub-a-scrubbing their collated 3-seme-
ster's-worth of mess

pull out the heating elements and wipe around the bowls, give
it one pass, two pass, still there's more, and you wonder why
you're doing this, cleaning after him, and your hands move
silently

· · ·

because it's something to do

keep from realising, that you're here alone

18

So let's say there is a Hero. And he is young.

His uncle thinks him an eyesore, and so the Hero is ordered away on a seemingly insurmountable quest. But this Young Hero has been gifted with charisma and the knack of getting others to do what he wants.

Hestia: "Really, what *do* you see in that boy though"

Hera: "I can't help it; he's just so handsome..."

The Hero is out on a Quest, which means he is looking for convenient women to do his chores for him. The Hero and his men come to an island of recently widowed girls, with teary eyes and pretty faces and ○○○. Promises are made, vows of ever-lasting love, and then a whole lot of hot-and-steamy *that*. And, when it comes time to leave, the girls all find themselves believing. They have forgotten their dead husbands and the broken promises and all are thinking "this time... this time maybe it can work".

"Don't forget about me, ok?"

"I won't!", he says.

(He does.)

• • •

Hero on a mission, sailing here and sailing there. When trouble comes there is no shame in running far away, or else in delegating it to one of his followers to handle. After all, a Hero is not at all like the bits of Theseus' ship, or like the galley slave members of its crew. The Hero's role is as a figurehead, and so he cannot be replaced.

They come at last to their final destination, and the Hero tries negotiating with the old king. He prattles on for hours, laying the charm in heavy sheets, before finally getting around to asking: "can we please take away the prize?".

It is no good. This old man does not like boys.

Who does like boys?, he looks around... Ahah!, the daughter does! And she is smitten in an instant (whether love-struck or god-struck who can say) and knows that she will give anything for him. A daughter who betrays her father for this beautiful boy, telling all for the chance to feel his fingers ruffling her hair. He casts a spell on her and then she casts a spell in turn, lays the path for him to take what is Rightfully His.

This story has repeated through more times than you can remember, from first γλυκύς to last πικρός, start to end. And it's happening even now, right now out there today, this when and many somewheres a Hero is sailing out to sea, and the girl (or boy) is left stranded on an island, and the food is running out.

"Eternal ephebe", when Heartlessness is innocent and gay, and every Lover is expected to be Mother, is replaced with someone new.

19

you are becoming insatiable

you wake and you are reading, in the shower, out the door.
you read and, while you're reading, you are finding things to
read, drown your mind with disembodied voices, give yourself
to them, borrowed-feeling, psychic-distance, shelter-shroud

a castle or a prison has to do with point of view

dazai says that people read as a response to loneliness. wal-
lace says that writing is the same. to you the use of words is
not connecting but concealing, don't let anybody see you, self
included, self-the-most

there is a little place at work, you hide-away-with-books, a little
corner in a corner, in the knook behind a shelf, 読み隠し,
spirited away

ganymede, sing, in a thousand-lives exchange for stolen-one

· · ·

and so library job is gone as well then, well...

84

1a

walking home one day, and you are reading while you walk.

the rabbits are in season, and they run when you come near, and you find that you are chasing them and catch one in the corner of a wall, and there's an instinct that you don't quite understand, but that you're smiling to yourself, and in the deep inside your throat there is a sound that might be laughter or a growl

.   .   .

walking home one day, and your shadow starts to lengthen. the sun goes down, and, soon enough, you're walking in the dark. the street lamps give a length to you; you grow and shrink and grow, until you reach the last and don't stop growing; only you dissolve, and then your shadow is the dark, and so are you

1b

nov 2 1

esther moved out

paid off the lease and left while i was gone. she must have seen us last weekend. well, that's fair

not sure what to do from here, try to find a job and place at the same time. money's running out

• • •

i don't know what day it is

at least it isn't hot; still need to drink more

a wash is a good place to sleep. it is a good place to hide a blanket, tuck it up under a bushy tree that hasn't been pruned to stand, a change of clothes inside. it is a place to not be seen

leave a few things there, a blanket and spare change of clothes

books i keep wrapped up in plastic, then inside a duffel bag i guess that's called. thankful for the first time that it doesn't rain often the park in this neighbourhood has got a faucet meant for dogs, head over at night to clean my hair and things. need to watch for the teens who hang around trading drugs, but nothing really dangerous. food will be a problem soon but a transaction:

- you receive: me
- i receive: money
- money becomes: food
- food becomes: me

self-assembly line, conveyor belt

party-favour, gift-exchange. appetiser, finger-food. tides you over till the evening meal

close your eyes and close your ears and close your mind away, you are not here, you are living Somewhere Else

a stranger is inside you feels like you are being erased

cross you out with a big fat X, a stranger wears your face

hello, my name is batsuko, and i'll be your you to-day

we *do* so hope that you enjoy your stay

. . .

think, mcfly, hellóòoo, is there anybody home?

pulling back the bolts and chains and opening the door

distraction

interaction

everyone is happy here, all smiles

avoid speaking directly yeh?, some things just aren't said

a transaction:

- i receive: money
- i receive: you

1d

"you *know* not to bring that shit in here, mán. take it some-
where else, ok? we're done"

the room is over-packed and warm, and you begin to sweat.
12 metres squared, and humans sprout like corn from every
inch, gently wavering in waves that run from corner out and
back again and interfere into a mess of bodies bumping bodies
bumping you

Mr. Proprietor, he ushers out a pair of teenage boys, in shirts-
too-large and torn-out-knees and crooked-faces-looking-down,
the one tight-clutching-close a paper bag and looking rather
sheepish, rather vulnerable, rather easy prey, and you feel your
fingers start to twitch, and you quickly look away

beside you is the curly mop who wanted you to come, showed
you pictures, white-and-black and some a faded blur-of-fog,
showed you music, showed you what he wants to be, and has
he got so much enthusiasm, feel a mother's urge, this little
puppy bouncing in his combat boots and denim vest, and so

you came here to protect him as he grows

weeks later, when he meets someone, it feels a sending-off.

"take care of him, ok? or else"

        •   •   •

from back of all the bodies, you are standing on your toes. you catch her eye. you catch her.

sarah,

is sixty six inches tall, has a straight-blonde-crop, cut-short

all-black all-year, wears a loose-knit over-hands long-sleeve-pull, yarn-coarse

is very warm, and smells of soap from the bar

trace your fingers down her arm, budump budump, a-lined in white and collagen, "because it's just a fucked up thing to do, you know?"

will surprise you in the shower, reach and grab you from be-hind. will surprise you any-where, every-time

rubs her blood under your eyes and says your name, calls you prarie dog and "hey, tall thing" and dude

disappears

       .   .   .

and in this way, passing in and out of time

days are gone to blurring, one thing comes after another all so
quickly, and your world is shrunken down

to sleep in unfamiliar places pulls the world unmoored; three
metres cubed is all the world there is to you, focus now, can i
sleep here, can i eat here, is it time to be moving on

a heightened sense of other peoples faces, need to read them
in a moment, keep a mask to hide your own

there were some men there then and you went with them, went with the dark and heavy men, you went with them, you were there and there were some men were them

and you were gay there then, not very gay then, just gay then

and there were some women then, and dark and heavy men, and some of the women were dark, and some of the men were not so heavy, and sometimes it was dark and you were together then, you were with the women and men

and you were with them then, and you were not where you wanted to be, with them, the dark or heavy, women or men, and you went to another place and stayed there

and you left them then. and you went to another place and stayed there. in the day there.

and you sleep now, when the sun is out, and night is where you live

if

protectress of lighters and box-stored wine. beef jerky, ch'arki, protein in plastic. dehydrated salinated. deoxyginated.

spiritless strips of lifeless lump. nothing spoils in this dump.

ch'arki, that's from quechua. nahuatl words are best. chili and chicle and chocolate. chilpoctli mōlli. āhuacatl tomatl. coyōtl. coyōtl.

the bell, and up you look, and it's what seems a happy couple, and they're here like everyone: "the drinks are out and all the stores are closed and haven't you got anything a little nicer?" "no, i'm sorry, that's the all of it, though maybe try that beer, the orange one, that one is slightly palate-able, yeh", and they are smile and gone and you're alone again, and you are read-ing, with your book under the counter, with your book, under the counter you are reading with your book, time is ticking, time is ticking you are ticking, time is ticking you are you.

• • •

the inca

are a puzzle, so they say

with words like "loosely-coupled", "multi-cultural", and "iso-
lated settlements", the king himself can shine on only one lo-
cale at once

divide to conquer, sure, except it was a strategy repeatable. by
bearded pales, with fingers full of gold

the inca

they are distant, far away

the first of written records by a native, it was written out three
quarters of a century beyond the death of emperor-the-last

accounts are biased terribly, in one way or another. utopia
of daemons and a savage land of plenty. they conquered
peacefully, except for when they slaughtered thousands in the
higher parts of ecuador and turned a lake to red

bone fed. lake bed. mud bled. blood red.

the variant in ecuador, that's kichwa, is further from the origin
than any other kind

(or maybe not)

. . .

the inca

they are speaking

the inca, they are dead and they are speaking

the dead, and they are speaking and are going out for parties
and for tea, out to call on other bodies and complain about the
mess, the kids these days

complain about the mess you all have made, made a mess all on
the lawn outside my window, where i liked to sit and watch
the seasons change, made a mess of all the seasons, burning
bush and acid rain, made a mess out of the sky, and now the
nights have all gone grey, and where's Yacana disappeared to?,
someone sound the harvest chime, and our future has gone
empty, and we've lost the track of time, and my grandchildren
resent me, and it's all a load of slime, a coat of grime

ch'arki for 5 quarters and a dime; keep the change. and build
on top of it, your buildings squash our bodies flat

20

the train, at 1am, is bright and dirty, sterile and dark

the darkness walls you in, this day-bright room of sagging bod-
ies, and you close up your umbrella, shake it lightly, water
frees

a woman and a man look up to see you, look away

tan coats hide tanning bodies, greying hair and greying eyes,
and they fold up that more tightly in a tempt to hide their
gently-burning cores, hide their aching and their sores, next
stop now, rain and open doors, and here's this man who is
a crag of tattoo chest and narrow eyes, sits beside the folded
couple and they both get up to move, and now it's you here is
beside him and your body, feel your body anymore, then a gap
in your awareness and you're curling in a corner, on the floor,
and your shaking lets them see you, and there is no place to
hide

"she's got a history, that one"

you are a thing in a museum, and they wonder how you work,
and just who was it has made you, and just why

. . .

because the floor was wet, so you got a little wet on the seat
of your jeans, means that now you're awkwardly because they
stip with every step, and so you get a bit away from the train's
stopping area and then you sit again, in a bit more wet, and
star up at the stars, and there are cloud makes it impossible,
but you don't really care

it starts to rain a little, and there's water in your hair

a man in a crumpled suit, standing on the sidewalk, looking frustrated and turning here and there as people bend and slide around him as an obstacle and push ahead. twilight starts to drop, but there's no colour here for it to suffocate, concrete buildings, concrete walkways, asphalt roads, and the man himself in black and white and patches dirty grey, blending in so no one sees him, subcomponent of the city, bit of noise in its compression, lossy artefacts outside of their perception, he can safely be ignored

well-worn cog sprung loose from the machine

you're back some 60 paces from the crowd, and so you reach him all alone, and he is waiting for you there

"So where are you off to, then?". acid smile. notice me

"trying to find somewhere to stay"

"Oh... I'm sorry."

"no, it's fine"

.   .   .

there was a man, a fair bit drunk, came on the train one day.
he was frustrated and angry; he was hurt

he looked at me and said "get off our land", and i wondered
what it meant and where he wanted me to go

i have never been to norway; i have never been to prussia;
frozen worlds, thousands of miles away, hundreds of years ago,
peoples and languages that no longer exist

i was born 10 miles from here. if this is not my land then what
land is?

.   .   .

面汚し者め、honour killing (whose?)

a girl who says "can i please be your daughter", father beats
her over the head, with a toaster, laid out on the kitchen floor

a girl looks over the side of the bridge, too dark to see the water
down below, puts down her bag, takes off her shoes and gloves
and lines them up all neatly

goodbye

the family can find a good story to tell when people come
around asking. she will not even be a statistic

people drift into your life and then are gone again, and you
have never yet been to a funeral, 他人 takes them all away

. . .

changeling births

strangers in a familiar land, we have been displaced

we have no culture, history; we have no family

"invert", "pervert", this "half" is new to whom?

"asegi", a novelty we are.

will we live or die?, were we ever here at all? decision making
all is up to you

22

Now, there came a day when Pandora's Gifts presented them-selves before her, and Fear was also among them. And she asked, "Where have you come from?". And Fear replied, "From you".

And, with this revelation, she was sorely troubled, wondering if there might be a way to live a sentience without producing fear.

"Skin for skin!", replied her Fear. "In order to dispose of me, you must first be rid of yourself. For I am flesh of your flesh, and marrow of your marrow. Your people will be my people, and your thoughts my thoughts. And we will a–ll go together when we go∼♪♪. And to just one place, for we are of the dust, and so unto it shall return".

"Then I shall be rid of it", she said. "This self. Like the nymphs of old, in my escape I shall become something new. Not under the sun, but in the darker places".

And, just like that, she went

23

A strange woman beckons to her.

"That which swallows your heart, that hurtful sorrow, hurtful knowing. Come with me now and it will be erased."

心が迷ったら

観てもなんも見えない
聴いてもなんも聞けない
食べても味わえない

Down and down they go, walking the paths unto the dead. And, all her days, she eateth in the darkness and knows not what is her sorrow and her sickness.

横

24

Now, let me tell you another story.

Way out low in the Sonoran, and back when your mother's mother's mother still hadn't even been born, there lived a certain clever boy who had figured out how to ward off *onryou*, the vengeful spirits of the dead. This clever boy knew how to purify a building using salts, drawing them out in guarding lines and writing old symbols of power, and so it was he came to be known to people as the *Shioko*, meaning "Salt Child". And, along with his salts, the Shioko would always carry with him a beautiful wooden flute, and he would play this flute and then recite his poems, strange and otherworldly, which people called *shiotanka*, and in this way he could charm spirits and send them back into the earth.

Now this Shioko, from a very early age he left his home and went off wandering here and there, dispelling spirits and selling medicines and charms he learned to make along the way, because every village their mothers have got their own secret remedies, you see, and he would ask to learn from them as thanks for purifying their houses and their shrines. And so he would play his flute and grind his medicines and tell stories of all the places he had visited, and so charming was this boy that even the gods themselves would sometimes stop to listen to him then, slipping by unnoticed in among the audiences that were always gathered around him. And, in a little while, it was such that everybody in the whole world knew the name of Shioko, and anyone who needed help to fend away a vengeful ghost would send out word and he would come to them and help them. And things continued on like this a while. And everyone was glad.

But good things, you know they never last forever though, and soon enough there came a tragedy that people speak of even still today, and that is why I'm telling you this story now. It was early afternoon one day in the very heart of summer, one of those days when it gets so hot that even the animals all crawl into their dens and hide until the sun goes down again. So hot that, when you try to speak, even your words will shrivel up and die as they leave your mouth, and all your friends complain that the world sounds tinny and flat, and the only thing you hear is the sizzle of some poor lizard or snake who's stayed too long out sunning itself on a big black rock and is slowly starting to fry.

And, on a day like that, you bet that Shioko was stuck inside as well and was trying his very darndest to stay cool, and here he is fanning himself and sighing in despair because the sweat collecting all over his face was making his makeup start to run, and he was a little vain, you see, and couldn't ever go out putting on a performance without his makeup and hair and clothes all coming together *just* right, and maybe you can say that's something both a blessing and a curse, to have your standards always set so high that even Shioko, the prettiest and cleverest boy in all the world, even he sometimes still can't live up to them.

And so he's sitting at his mirror like that, and he's *hmm*ing and *haw*ing and fanning away and getting all desparate when suddenly... he starts to feel of a sudden that tingle-chill runs up and down your spine to tell a spirit's come visiting you. And he whirls around so quickly and he reaches for his flute, already whispering out the first words of a spell, only to find what's this, who's standing there behind him and with a crooked smile all bent in pain, it's the most beautiful girl that he ever saw and of anyone still has since. And this girl, she is *so* beautiful and has *such* a look of sadness about her that Shioko at once forgets all his tricks and all his vanity and he rushes over there quickly to her side. And she's standing there and crying, and he's asking "what's wrong, what's wrong", because of course he's the Shioko and he knows a spirit when he sees one, but this girl is just so beautiful and he's fallen at a single glance in love, and so he knows that he'll do anything for her.

And besides, he's thinking that this girl is so sad she can't be anything but an *urei*, or a spirit of sorrow. Because humans have got four souls, you know, and each of these has a name we give when it returns to the earth to carry out some business there. There is the *orei*, a spirit of gratitude that watches over as a guardian those who had helped and cared for the spirit in life. Then there are *kirei* of great strength and purity, from those who have lived well and give luck and blessings to whomever passes by, and the *onryou*, spirits of anger at having been wronged or slighted. And last of all is the *urei*, that's also called *yuurei*, which is the spirit of a person's grief that has been fueled by a great sadness.

And the girl who is an urei falls into his arms and weeps and weeps, and Shioko gathers her up and carries her to his bed to lay her down, which even for a boy so delicate proves easy because, as you may have guessed, that a one-fourth spirit only weighs one fourth of what a human does in life. And he waits there patiently until at last her tears are dried and she sits up and, stammering, begins to speak.

"My husband", she says. "The one I loved...

It was our wedding day, and all the preparations made. And my mother and father here in town to visit, and the family all together. we were so happy...

Ours had been a long-distance relationship, and all my

friends had said that sort of thing could never work, except i thought that here we are, and we're going to get married and prove all of them wrong, and he's come all the way to meet me here with his mother and father, come down from the great lakes and brought all these fancy gifts like i've never heard of before. We were so happy, my husband and I. We said our promises and drank the marriage wine, and there was music and we danced, and I saw my older sister-in-law, who's usually all grumpy and likes to fight, but even she was out there waltzing with my mother, and both stumbling and laughing and they're holding each other up, and I knew it then that everything in the whole world was all right and going to be the way it should, and in the future things could only get better.

And so we had our first night together and were sinking off to sleep, and I was drifting, thinking how handsome his half-sleeping face had been, that look of really being relaxed for the first time in the longest while, now that it all was over and everything beginning. And I was *just* about away when the annoying feeling everybody knows brought me back up again with a jerk, and I had to get up and go outside to do *that* (which anyways, after being together, they say it's important and healthy to do, you know?) and so I walked out into the desert a ways, and it's so beautiful at night, though there are snakes and scorpions, but just look up a second and you'll forget all that with how the sky spreads out and sucks you in and makes you feel so tiny small... My husband, where he came from way up north, he said they have trees and mountains and clouds, and so when he first came here he got so shocked and couldn't stop talking about how strange it was, and I can't help seeing it that way ever since.

And I'm crouching there after peeing, staring up at the sky and losing myself in thinking about these things, when someone I never even got to see comes creeping up behind me and just snatches it all away. And he beats me half to death and has some fun and drags me far out into the desert where no one will ever find me there, he says, and he's right, they never did... and I died out there, lying on my back and I can't move and all the stars are spinning spinning up above."

And it's at this point when her story is just about done that she starts to cry again, and Shioko, who's been listening so carefully, is brought to tears as well. And he sits there at the edge of the bed and brushes her cheek while she cries, and then she reaches up to take his hand into a finger fold and looks into his eyes, and they are quiet a while. Then the ghost woman starts to speak again, all hurried and rushed like she doesn't want to think about what she's saying and just wants it to be through.

"My future is over, just like that, and next thing I know

I'm back here on the earth but only as a spirit so nobody can even see me. And my husband... well at first he's rushing here and there and has all the family searching, but then in a while they're all done looking and crying and start heading off back to home. And because they never found any trace, and because of when it happened, my husband thinks I must have run away, that I didn't want to be with him but was too weak to say it. So then he got so hurt and angry, and all I wanted was to let him know the truth.

But of course you know how it is, that he's gone home again to the north while I'm stuck here where my body died and I can't ever see him again. So I came to you. Because from the work that you do I was certain that you'd be able to see me, even if no one else can. And besides that I've watched you a bit, and before you came heard all the people talking, and so I saw how much you care for people, even the ones who are completely strangers, and how you always have kind words and will drop anything to help. So I thought it could be ok, to trust you with this, because you're the only one who might be able to... to..."

But she can't finish speaking before she's pulled back into sobs. And together they cry and cry until they're both spent and the ghost girl falls asleep, and this is something that even Shioko didn't know, that a spirit could fall sleep without a body, because his experiences have all been with angry and vengeful onryou who were too busy chasing down and trying to eat people or to kill everything that moves, and so he doesn't rightly know what to do. So he leaves her there and walks over to a neighbour's place to spend the night with a friend.

Now but here's what else Shioko didn't know though, is that this beautiful girl was really the ghost of Ibari yamanbaba and an onryou, come back from the dead to get her revenge. That Ibari lived up a mountain way off to the east, and there she crafted powerful charms and brewed up fearsome potions of the kind you'd do right to be wary. She lived there a loong long time, taking on customers and callers and building up quite a reputation for herself, and with her tricks she kept her body looking all young and beautiful even though she was so old, and all together she was very pleased with how her life was going. Then one day, though, she notices that the line of customers that's always standing outside her door has suddenly gotten pretty short, and normally it would stretch on and wrap around down her few steps and into the garden, but this time there are only ten or so waiting right there outside her door, and two of those are a couple and will be wanting the couples' discount, and another is just her old neighbour probably come to complain again about the smells from all the potions and the tanning that she does out back as a little side-hustle now but that she's really been questioning recently herself because the smell is so bad.

And so she gets to thinking that maybe smell is why the crowd's so thin as well, but then she overhears the little girl of that annoying couple is whining away at her husband, saying things like "ah darling, why did we have to come here to this horrid old baba's house. I wanted to go see Shioko instead, isn't he dreamy?", and so from that Ibari yamanbaba, who you know was called so on account of she's so proud, that's how she finds out that she's got a rival out there somewhere, and that it's some kusogaki really cramping on her style. And from then on she wakes up every day to find there's fewer and fewer customers out there waiting in her garden, until in a little while she wakes up one day and there's no one out there at all, and from then on she spends her days all alone and lonesome up on the mountain, and picking out stitches and twiddling her thumbs and not even knowing *what* to do, until the stress just eats and eats away at her and she turns all bitter, or at least even more than she was before, and it gets to the point where all her time she's spending thinking about clever ways to get back at that jerk face Shioko, who's thinking he's so hot and stealing away all her customers so easily, and whatever happened to brand loyalty those marketing advisers were always getting on about. And it's so bad she starts to think that maybe life just isn't fair, and what's the point of having lived so long and now all she was living for has gone and abandoned her, and so she's thinking "I may as well die" and then she does, brews up a poison that's terrible strong and drinks it down in just one gulp and topples right over, *smack*, and moving not even a twitch, and no one ever comes to check on her there except some years later on a couple of kids who sneak in on a dare, and all they find by then is piles of dust and a few old lonely bones.

So that's the end of that!, is what you'd think but no, because her hatred was so strong that then a part of her came back as an onryou and hatched this clever plan for getting her revenge, just like Oiwa with that fruit Tamiya Lemon, to show him what it's like to be degraded and disgraced and have your whole life ruined by a person whom you've never even met. And she vows to find the Shioko and bring him along, back down with her to hell.

But Shioko knows nothing about all that, and all he sees is this crying, pitiful, and oh-so-lovely spirit here in front of him and wants to help her any way he can. So he sets off right that moment (well, he waits till the sun goes down so as not to be crisped) and off to find these lakes that his girl has told him about. And it's a reaally long way to walk, up over mountains and through the Great Plains, and all the way he's stopping by at little villages till everyone across the whole big continent knows who he is, and they're all waiting and so glad to see him visit when he comes.

And it goes on like that until he's way up north and just about reached the lakes, and it's gotten all cold up here and yellow-green and blue, and he's bundled up in furs and shiver-chattering and wishing he can hurry up and go back home to where the air is dry and there are no clouds in the sky and where every day is sun. And he catches his foot on a rock and nearly stumbles, and it's right about then, when he's sniffling and trying not to cry, when there's a man cuts out from behind a tree and right into his path.

This man is as tall as tall, so he looks to Shioko a bit like a walking mountain, and the very tip top of his head gone bald and shining like the snow. The two stand still a while, stare each other up and down. Then Shioko steps left, and the man steps left. And Shioko steps right, and the man steps right. And back and forth they go, left and right and here and there, so it starts to feel they're acting out a dance. And Shioko laughs, and the man looks to be a bit annoyed.

"Little girl", the coarse man says.

"I ain't a girl; I'm Shioko!"

"Little girl I ain't got time for this, now you come along quietly now, you hear? Or else you're thinking I should do something bout that pretty face of yours.", he says and makes a scary gesture with his fist. And so Shioko hasn't got a choice but to follow and see what this grumpy old man has got in store for him, so he goes.

Off the path and into the woods they walk, with Shioko got his hands bound up and tied and the man is following right on just behind him. It's starting to get dark and pretty cold, and Shioko's clothes are only things meant for the desert means he pulls his arms in to his sides and goes *buruburuburu*, not able to cross them with they're tied behind his back. And the watching man has got this smile on his face, like he's enjoying what he sees.

Now this is where the story starts to get a bit tough to tell, and maybe you can see where it's headed but I still got to let you know. So the dangerous man walks Shioko back to his camp, where he and all these other men are staying. And the men all look like him, even though their bodies are all different shapes, so that some are tall and fat and some are short and thin and you can see here and there bits and odd pieces of them are missing, but still they're all the same be- cause they've all got that look on their faces, that same smile that's about when something good has happened, and that it's bad for someone else. And when Shioko opens his mouth to speak they don't even let him start, but one of the men walks over and slaps him right there hard so that his face twists over to the side and then slumps forwards-down. Which starts the laughter up, so they're all shouting and laughing away, and even when someone unties him Shioko just stands there not even trying to move, shut away inside his head. Because, with all his charms and tricks and his experience with the dead, still he's never fought with a living human before and wouldn't know where to start

Then the dangerous man shouts "quiet" and the crowd falls into a hush. What the man has got to say of course is this, a story all about a pretty girl comes up to him and offers him a job (but he leaves out the part that he tries to get with her and gets a kick instead), and it's a simple job, just wait by the road til a traveller comes along is all dressed up and looking fancy and smug and needs someone to wipe that look off his face. And then (after some invented racey bits) she says "it's nearly time, so just wait right there, ok? And you can do it however you like, and after I promise that I'll make it worth your while.", which the man had thought is very fair indeed, "don't you all think?", and the others break into a laugh.

Betrayal! That oh-so-pitiful girl she never wanted his help at all, and from the start it was her plan that he should be trapped this way! And for the first time Shioko feels building in him some emotions that make him terrified, a hatred for himself, for the woman, for a stupid world that can let things like this happen to even people who try their very best to do things right and give back more than they've taken. And the hatred starts to steal away his body and his mind before he fights it down and tells himself to focus, that it's true this is a tricky situation, but there's no use giving up hope just yet, so he's got to keep his wits about and patiently wait for his chance.

"A chance, a chance, just one chance...", he's thinking all the way as they walk with him into the woods and to a place seems suitable enough to use, and they're all arguing over who gets first and second and who owes now what to whom and you're my kouhai still you know, show some respect. But finally it's sorted, and then one after another those men all take turns in doing what they will.

They leave him there tied up undignified, with his arms around front of the tree, and his head up in the clouds, and his spirit in the dirt. Some hours pass, and the air starts turning colder. Starts turning colder. Starts turning dark.

Buruburuburu.

He says it again and louder this time, *BuruBuruBuru*, not like he thinks it's something that can save him, but there's a name for that, like when an animal gets caught into a trap and starts to act compulsively, because you know at least that feels like doing something, and just the doing itself can be enough to keep your mind from seeing. So Shioko goes on shivering, in his exaggerated way, and the sun is dropping down behind the mountains and it's getting ever colder and he's wondering how long hypothermia takes, if it's like heat stroke how it makes you just keel over and die well then that's got to happen soon then, hasn't it?, seeing as he's so cold already now and his hands are going numb. And it's just about he's thinking that and the light is just about gone when he starts to hear the shouting of the wolves.

And it's a sad thing, but in the end he became that very thing he'd spent so long on trying to protect people from, an onryou, and maybe the most dangerous of them all, because he knew all the tricks there were to banishing and how they all could be avoided.

He came to hate all women and men and everybody who was still alive and having fun, resented them for all the things he wanted most and couldn't have, a happy and productive life and a handful of people they could love and things to work on, goals they could go chasing after. So he started to find ways that he could trick them, and he'd stir up hopeless jealousy and longing and would push people *just* right so that in the end they would betray either each other or at least themselves and give up living and would pass on into death. But there was another part of him too that was so painfully sad, and it stayed right there with that body he could never have again, that beautiful corpse that's missing pieces turned eventually to dust and then to nothing left at all. And even now on quiet nights there, if you listen hard enough, you just might hear him singing one of those shiotanka, not so strange anymore but only sort of hollowed out and empty, and he sings:

people who you love
all those things you think you know
they can be erased

this was all so long ago
this was all so far away

Or:

cheer is gone from me
always i am lonely here
in this land of grey

just once more, i want to see
lord apollon's smiling face

For a long time after, then, mothers would tell their children the story of Shioko, the wiliest and most fearsome of all the onryou. And, after these stories had been told many times, the words began to shift, and people began to think of all vengeful returning spirits as *shioko*. These days it is said that someone who has died a lonely or jealous death, or one under violent circumstances, that person can sometimes come back to our world as *shioko* and look for happy people to bring down with them into the Lands of the Dead. And so it is that when a person dies we leave out food for them, and wine, because a contented spirit is a spirit who will pass on peacefully.

gone underneath to see the other side of the world, beneath the hills, find a way down between the rocks a squeeze, and over the river by bridge. i wonder has it got a true name, not sanzu or styx but something really all its own, because this land of human-dug canals is not reliant on your foreign gods, human created and maintained

dark it is, these halls are damp and growing, overflown deposits of trogloxenenic composting, detrivorous decomposition, sapro-myco-phyto-ghastly-white, borrowed carbon will be paid, paid in time. a closed-loop web stretched here to there and back, a maximal clique of reciprocal catabolites, the living are the dead. feel my way 手探り until there's a bit of glow, luminescence on the walls, someone has grown in patterns here, drawn out words and images in a nutrient stew, somebody seems who wants to always be reminded, it says in letters softly glowing that: "there is no one up there for you now. do not forget"

who can it be?, would write something so sad, or maybe bitter is the word, or maybe more astringency, reacting to an assault pulls inwards and away

• • •

tunnels forking, turning curves. this place is large. something
about layered ecosystems, walk a few feet in and it's another
world, will-o-the-wisp feed lampenflora, then just feet away
are empty eyes and brush-antennae, made to see the dark

wandering for hours finding no one but the animals, are
the animals a someone, undecided on this point

down and down through microcosms, stirrings in the deep,
where mirror-worlds of subspecies have lost their terrestrial
mechanisms, translate, mutate, rearranging, SNIP SNIP. envi-
ronments as error-corrective checksum-calculators, evolution
at the interface, can't be too loosely coupled, generics make for
over-engineering make for quickly-starving, even if they don't
degrade from underuse. luckily for them broken is a relative
term. now where's my vitamin c

find it then, i've stumbled on, a single-tenant hermitage,
and gosh how it's dark in there. somebody lives inside grown
up a house of troglobiont fungi, somehow frozen, neither fruit-
ing nor dissolving, someone frozen in the past

• • •

the woman hasn't got a name, so at least she says, is an ever-
present-presence in this place

this is a world is written in reverse

sky above is empty, glitter stars are in the dirt, holding hol-
low sparks of memories that no one now can hear

pick a bone the dusty earth has sparkle at its heart, and
the surface brased smooth to the touch, run a finger down the
river-washed length borne up to the bank, are the dead who
have been lost

too poor

what can be done?

26

a shadow

she says to you "come with me now;

i've something you should see"

• • •

listen.

can you hear it?

they say that someone fell here, when the banks were river-run

they say there was a flooding, and the boy was drowned in
seconds

they say that he was knocked unconscious, head against the
rock; they say "he thought he was invincible"; they say that he
was young

they say

the boy, his name was jacob, and he was a boy beloved. was out there with his brother, running circles, being dumb. they say that he had eggs for breakfast, left his room a mess, used to sleep with both dogs at his feet, despite his mother's warnings, used to drink milk from the gallon, used to track mud on the carpet, toss his schoolbooks in the corner, left unread

used to call his mother names, and then apologise and try to make her smile, try to tell her that he didn't really mean it, that it hadn't been her fault and that he hated that guy and they were better off this way, without him in the end

the end

the ending, it was swift, but not so quick as they had thought. he didn't hit his head too hard until some seconds later, man- aged for a while to hold his breath and had the time to think, had the time to realise that he was here and here was some- where he was never coming back from and his brother had to watch, and his mother couldn't watch, and he was going and that was the full of it

a spectacle but nothing strange, a single hurt mother and an arrangement of the system not worth pointing he asked you to tell her: "it wasn't on purpose"

he asked you to give her: "hope"

you tried, but you've forgotten how; the words have all es-
caped you, and the people mostly run now, when they see
you, or they hope that you will do

that you will do

·　　·　　·

黄泉

本読み

毒素　読書　<ruby>土<rt>ど</rt></ruby>

nowhere to go, you read the past and let the future slips away,
order sense from disarray, cut away, cut clean

（地下）

the woman in the dark, she shows you secrets, hidden pieces
of yourself, how a person can be free

"alive up there, they need us.

but we do not need them."

138

27

she the woman tells a story

as we are here in the world, and as the time is passing and my hair is growing ever longer, we are learning just a little all the time, and so it feels perhaps it might be worth to tell a bit the story of events that are the measure of our days, it being so that days themselves are measured only in our passing and our time

二人暮らし

then to begin, there is beside me here a man who is the other to my one, is the one who gives a balance to my path so that together we are one as two, in time and space apart but in all else we are a unit, as a counterweighted scale, and ours the task of marking progress for the many who take from us both their energy and rest. an act of balancing, give and take and share more freely, freely mingling our motions and our feelings so to stabilise the world that is awash with so many faces, and relying on our motions and our regularities to be a measure for their wisdoms and a marker for their days but under all this outwardness there is an us as well who are a quiet-living solitude where only we can go, and watch the mountains slick with rain comes down to meet us here to grow a tended garden for the meals we share, and single bed and single chair, with spaces perfect fitted so the bath has room for two and just enough that legs can tangle comfortably

and so he becomes sick i care for him, and i need a new comb he carves from a heart of ironwood and says "now this, it cannot break ever again", and it feels a little while just so, that there are some things can't be broken, and that we are one of them

分裂

until there is a day we sit together gaze the garden, dangle feet over the deck and share our kayu as an easy-frugal breakfast, rubbing sleep from each other's eyes and feel the gentle morn-ing breeze dances the roses into view. and then of a sudden he says "you are a flower, so pleasant to me", and i ask "ahah, then are you a bush? ah no, i think that you should be a flower with me, and that way we make a pair", and the thought of us as flowers gently waving in the breeze, it feels so cheerful that i cannot help but smile, but then i see him only staring down below, and with a furrow in his brow and so it is that quite soon after he appears before me, and there is a confrontation rather pointed, catches me somehow aware but unprepared, says "well, i am a man, you know, and you are not, and we are thus to be uneven then it does not feel right to me, continuing on pretending so when anyone can see, and all the people do, you hear them talking, and please don't be unreasonable, you know there is only just so much that a man can take"

and it comes to me in that moment that he is jealous, can't i be the star and you my artemis, feels the words that are un-spoken, and despite trying to make light of the matter and to bring a smiling or a laugh, but in this uncomfortable manner further days are slowly passing, and our sharing draws apart until across the sky it is, and never comes to light when i am there and earth below lain out between us far

and i am a person as well, you know, not only something to reflect

なげきつゝ

i am lost. what is there to say, at such an impasse of wills, and what he wants, even in the case that we should meet again, but in that case the thing he wants only destroys us all the same, and wishing to show this to him i begin to write:

なでしこか　　　　"nadeshiko" you said,
もうあきなれど　　but it is autumn now
きてくれぬ　　　　and i find myself alone
こさめのこどく　　lonesomeness of little rain
はもきもくさる　　leaves and spirits fall again

though i realise that to show him these such self-indulgent words can only be fruitless, and i fold it up away and then lay down again, this empty-sided bed. and so.

and so to be always alone this way when one is one of two, to be alone is not a feeling felt before, is not a preparation for the shatter-heart sensation runs my heart to spine and out to toes and fingers cold so that i shudder, close-pull rigid cover shake

明るい未来

but a one must learn to live, and so i do, and say the same to you, do not be one who wants of anything, a radiant whole, we can shine

28

out running

you collect their bones

you go out

at night, the pile of bones, and you collect them, and you bring
them back for burying, beneath the joshua trees

splintered femur; baby teeth

the places where you bury them up spring new trees that sing
old songs together, and in this way you feel of use

preserve the essences of life, nothing forgotten, integrated syn-
thesis, entangled without loss

you dig into their memories and further from yourself, and you
are listening, and they are here inside you now and echoing,
as voices in the dark

.   .   .

were-uose-kamui, latransanthropy (gyny), living life in parallel
and independently

you are never hungry now

you are proud of your long-thin-legs. they let you run and run
and never get tired. you are proud of your strong jaws, "if you
need something, go out and get it". no more contingencies, no
more the awkward looks when you wait in line and someone
other disapproves, no more the worry over rules or rejections
or recalls, and won't you please fill out this form and sign your
name, but there's no way to stop somebody has got legs and
feet and 意志 and not one of them are owned

and you can sing. like never in your life, you can sing

29

"identity", a monoid both initial and terminal
a nowhere, self-containing self-sustaining
an end

"productivity", greedy humans, teōcuitlatl, silver-and-gold
gathering up treasures on the earth

"tradition", is identity but by another name
for people hate those whom they most resemble

only the dead can know the peace of distance from these crutches
a moment's quiet thinking to themselves

celebrate their passing, joy in sorrow
these three, i do not need them, and without them i am free

2a

"And I thought this needed to be brought before the rest of the congregation today, because this is a problem I've been dealing with as well. And it just wouldn't feel right to me; I believe that this is how God wants us to speak to one another, openly and honestly."

the pastor's face is earnest, and he moves his hands expressively. this is a speech he practised, in the mirror, when his wife was not at home

he wanted it to be as new to her as all the others

"Because the truth is that we *all* are sinners. We *all* have fallen short of the glory of God. And if I am to be your pastor, to be there when you need to confess your sins, then it's only right that you should all hear my confession as well."

the other men come join him, one by one up on the stage. one is crying, and another pulls him close, just briefly, from the side, for a moment and its gone

147

"All of us here, me included, have agreed to install a program that will send our browser histories to each other every month. This is about accountability, so we can be each others' strength, moving one step closer to a life like Jesus led."

.   .   .

takes until they've finished praying, and the crowd begins to break, before at last you pull your eyes away and leave the stained glass window and the parking lot of mini vans and station wagons, cut across the road and chase the sun until its right up overhead, and then you lay you down to sleep

dreaming of things you feel safe now remembering

but only memories and cut-away is . . . what?

an isolate is insulate. is it anything at all?

you stand up on the mountain ridge, look out over the city in the dark. a cross-hatch swim of glow

2b

days without the sun

days without the sun

morphisms

unspun

this is free this is

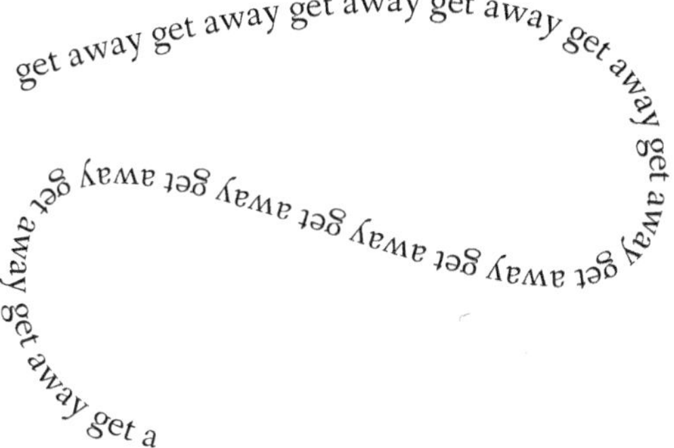

this is

which way

どこへ

2d

two in the dark, one two, is a novelty, gosh has it been a long
time

careful. careful now

the woman, though she has a strong face, but what does she
feel

living as a dead thing, 偽者じゃん, says the little voice not-
quite-erased

• • •

迷子迷子、 *are you free?*
they go i go, 同じ？
隠れん坊、 *can this be?*
signs of lacking, やる気？

in the world *is of the world*
even you don't *love the world*

little voice whispers true

153

"Tell us the one about the divine twins!"

"All right all right. Well now, how did it go..."

It was a loong time ago, way back before you or I or anyone we've ever known was born. Way back at the beginning of the world.

Back then, Old Earth was lonely. The world was always dark, and Earth had no way to pass the time. Every day it sat there in the dark, all alone, feeling the world slowly rotating in its place and the days proceeding, one after another, without changes that could mark them apart. Just how long things went on this way nobody can say. For ten years or ten thousand, the world was all so empty back then that even if you'd been there you'd be just as uncertain about it as me, which is to say that you wouldn't have a clue. And then one day all that changed. And that's because, after what had felt to it like a-ges and a-ges, Old Earth decided finally that it had had enough. And it said to itself: "This is no good at all! I am too lonely here, in this endless world of darkness where nothing happens but the passing of time that crawls on its way so slowly as to not be felt at all. And so, because I am so lonely, I will make myself some children who can help me feel more present and will give my life some purpose. And then maybe, when I'm old and when time finally passes me by, these children will be here to care for me as well.".

And with that Earth went out to find its very finest clay, and when it had found some it started to mould out people in all sorts of different shapes. It made squished people and stretched-out people and people shaped like pretzels until finally it found a shape it thought it liked the best. And then it formed another with that shape and breathed some life into them, because Old Earth has got the power of life, you know.

And so they were alive. "Ah, but somehow . . . hmmm", Old Earth was thinking, "I think that somehow they are still not quite right. They ought to be unique, with differentiating features, and then, because they're different, it will give them something to talk about with each other.". And Earth said to its two children: "Hey, you two; I've decided that it's best if one of you should be a woman and the other one a man. But, because it's such a big commitment, why don't you decide on which will be which?". And the twin on the left said "I will be woman", and the twin on the right said "I will be man". And so it was they were, Sister Sun and Brother Moon. And Old Earth was happy, that its children were so beautiful. And it told them so, and they were happy too.

Well, so for a while then Earth was quite content. Every day its children would go up to light the sky and then come down again and rush on back to home, and there Earth was waiting for them to tell them stories of the ancient times, before the world was made, of burning stars and roiling clouds of dust and lonesome emptiness and bits of rock come together to comfort each other then to break apart again. And, when finally it ran out of things to tell, Earth started to invent new stories, this time stories about people, villains and heroes and dangerous beasts, and then about little families living in little earthen houses, grinding corn and telling stories of their own. And from this Earth got to thinking that maybe that would be a good idea, that it could make some little people and have them try to live these tales like in a diorama or a play. "It could be an art project", thought Old Earth, "and something like a motivation; cause I've read that every thinking creature needs to have its passions in order to go on daily existing and stay positive and sane, and so maybe this could be mine".

So with that Earth made it that all around the irregular celestial spheroid there were humans that began to spring up out of caves and holes in the ground, and they came out as great sages or as warriors and laid claim to the patches of land beneath their feet. And they lived and worked, traded and fought and died, and so in time they got to be a little bit more like the humans that we know today, living packed together like termites in their overcrowded villages and cities. And in total some 3 million years were passed this way until Old Earth, who was by now starting to get a little bored and anyways feeling awfully tired, turned its face up to heaven and said "ah well, I think that that's enough work for now" and gently laid itself down for a rest. And you know it's stayed that way, sleeping, ever since.

Earth lost itself to dreaming... although not always peacefully, because it *has* been getting on in years and just about now to where it can wake itself up from angry coughing fits, due to the sleep apnoea you see, and which is why we have all these volcanoes and geysers that can explode and such these days. But so Earth lost itself to dreaming, and its children, those divine twins, they looked at their parent and then at each other and wondered what they ought to be doing with their lives, now that they were all alone. And so it was decided they should check in with the humans, those avtóhthones, and give them a few pointers on existing, cause they're thinking we learn best the things we teach. And on a certain mountain top they started up a school, though later it became known as a temple, and there they held each-weekend lessons for anybody who would come, free of charge, so that soon enough the entire mountain had become crawling over with excited humans all wanting to just get a glimpse of that shining pair of ancient twins they'd heard so much about, and people who then brought back with them an unexpected first-rate education, or at least what passed for one back in those days, before exchange programs and post-docs and the New Deal.

And what those humans learned about was this. From Brother Moon the humans learnt that every night is different and will bring a different danger, and that minds should be guarded jealously against corrupting influences, to always remind their children "what goes in must also come out". And Sister Sun, she told them about curiosity, that a strange first touch might burn, but there is often something good that's to be had on the other side, hidden clearings in the wood if you are brave enough to look. The humans took these contrary views to heart and tried to live their lives in balance, and in this way they came to flourish.

But that's a funny thing you know, that oftentimes those people who are so good at giving us advice are not themselves the best at putting it to practice, and those teachings that had been such a big help to the humans had at the selfsame time been drawing out a schism between those twins, who each thought their own way was the only way and that the other was at best a little naïve. But this was just in their deepest hearts that they were feeling so, down deep and covered over in places well beneath articulation, and anyways still only a little thing of the sort comes out in a tiff here and there but then seems quickly to be resolved, and so the true extent of the damage went unrecognised, a slow-festering wound.

And the twins grew older, and believed themselves wiser, and though they were always together, but this feeling still was growing till their actions all were painted over in a sense of vague unease. And when the pain had grown beyond their ignorance they packed up all their things and moved to a pair of separate little houses, river-riven by a valley in between.

It was difficult for them.

For those two, who had been always stuck together since they were born, living apart was a new kind of loneliness, and in order not to feel it they buried themselves away in separate pursuits, as while they had been together each acted to the other as a tether and a dampening force, so that cut free they sprung apart in mind each to their own extremes.

Without her brother there to scold her, Sister Sun freely indulged in all her secret pleasures and her fantasies, telling stories, chasing ghosts, and getting into trouble. And through it all she would always bring along one or two companions from the valley, of those people who'd come to be very dear to her, and if you're both very good then maybe I'll tell you my favourite of her stories some day, that's about the time she was captured by pirates and two little children of just your ages risked their lives to save her. But that's another tale for another time.

And, without his sister to poke at him, Brother Moon hid himself away in dark corners and sat motionless and studied little things, close-recordings of the forming-up of crystals and the breaking-down of foods into their block-component pieces, lysing cells and splitting acids and all manner of catalytic activities. And there would be some times he would go days without speaking a word, only absorbing what was written in strange texts acquired from hermits like himself. And in this way like certain monks he was never at risk of anything, whatever the thing in question might be.

And now you can probably guess that the story can't just end with things like that, these two careening away from one another at greater and greater speeds, so there was a day and a certain event that brought the conflict to a head, and it began, of course, with instigator Sun. Days passed, and Sister Sun had grown with each day ever closer to those humans in the valley whom her brother had so distanced himself from, and in time she found that she loved one of these humans most of all, so that this loved one occupied nearly all her waking thoughts, and though no word is left of how this human felt for her in return, or if they ever even exchanged a word, but Sister Sun's attachment was such that she would write of it in her diary and talk of stealing glances when she brought over gifts she made for her loved one's mother, or when she saw this person working in the field the way most people did those days, knee-deep in river water running or moving dirt from here to there. But then it came of a sudden the one she loved grew acutely ill and died, and this was such a shock to her that it changed everything.

For a year, Sister Sun was in mourning, which is the opposite of morning, though the second sometimes follows from the first. And the morning that came to Sister Sun was nothing bright but beaten over hard and flat with sadness, for she had seen now those three sights no person ever can unsee. And coming out of it she made a promise to herself that what was left of her own life she'd dedicate to find a way to conquer death and end the suffering of those humans whom she'd come to find so dear, the lives of whom were like a ripple in a wave, passing from one state to another always changing. And she remembered then her brother Moon, who surely in all his learning must have found a way of countering the process of decay. And she called out to him thus:

"Oh my brother, oh my brother won't you come out from your hiding place and help me? These people are suffering, and I don't know what to do, but you who have read so many things you must know a method that will prevent their deaths and that can make them young and well again."

And Brother Moon, who in this time had grown disused to movement and brightness, took a long while in answering her, flexing his knees and crawling out from where he was hidden and blinking blindly in the light. But with all this he settled down and answered his sister in turn, saying, "Sister, though I know it is your nature to be doing so, but this is why you must not get involved with people, for what you've now done is to build up earthly attachments and cling to them when you know these things can only pass away. Won't you instead come here and sit with me? Learn to clear your mind of feeling and only observe, 非思量, let nothing pass behind the boundary of your heart. Even though such a change would not come naturally to you, but it would be better if you learned to be like me and to mind your own business, and that way you won't have anything to worry about.".

But Sister Sun could not mind her own business. She was too taken with those poor people who had looked up to her, and she felt bound by the promise she had made. And so it was that very night she decided, that if Brother Moon would not help her then she'd find someone who would. And so she left her home on Earth and went to look.

Out out, far away, across the sky she went, hopping from star to star and asking after anyone who might know the secret to subverting entropy and death. And every place she went the answer found there was the same, that they had never heard of such a method and felt doubtful it could exist.

But even so, though it seemed the whole of our great galaxy could give no answer to her that she would accept, but the idea came that perhaps its princess twin and larger sibling might have something else to say. And with a subtle dance of arcs and gravity assists she crawled away from our great well, out through the milky halo, past globular clusters streaming, and towards the streak of light that was that far off ruler of men.

But Sister Sun had underestimated just how long a journey it would be, and she alone out there in the void with no one around but a few stray high-energy particles too quickly gone to even say hello goodbye. And the loneliness began to eat at her, nibble nibble, peel away light-particle-layers until she had only metallics left, and of those a precious few. And this is a way that even a sun can die, that if they lose the will to live they can be eaten up by darkness that's inside them grown too heavy to resist (well yes, but that depends on mass, but let's not worry about that). And she was alone out there, without a friend to feed her shining, and so the darkness grew . . . and ate her up . . . and snuffed her out.

·　·　·

Now at that time Brother Moon was of course hid in his hideaway and, as the sort of thing he did, calmly watching while a bunch of strawberries were slowly decomposed into botrytis grey and warm mush. But when his twin's light went out he felt it, and he looked away and thought to himself "I told her, didn't I?". And then a wave of emotion like he hadn't felt in many years came over him, and he stretched out flat on his back and rubbed those crater eyes that had given up on blinking and tried desperately to cry. But no tears came, his water being frozen down beneath the surface and locked there long ago. And presently the feeling passed, and Brother Moon sat up and began to form a plan for what he had to do.

And he left his hideaway and came to that place that some say is at Acheron, or else in Izumo, or at the bottom of a lake, but that wherever it is they all know what, that it's a gate leads down to that place kept deep under The Earth, where all the dead are restless-wandering in shallowness and grey. And at that door he knocked, and waited for his sister to answer.

The dead are slow, and Sun was slower still, so weary from her journeying, but her brother knew if anything how to wait, and he sat at that gate cross-legged for many turnings of The Earth. But when at last he heard a faint rustling and knew her to be just there, at the other side of the gate, then he quickly began to speak.

"Oh sister, oh my sister, look at what the world has done to you. Oh look at what pursuit of earthly things has done to that body that was once shining so brightly, but that now is all caught up in dark shade. I ask you, is it yet too late to change? Won't you turn away from all this foolishness and take a place with me and sit as my right hand in an eternal peacefulness like we were always meant to be, for hasn't this darkness been a suffering enough?"

But Sister Sun replied to him, in a dry and cracking voice, "It is so, I am in the darkness here, and it is very lonely, and it hurts. But even so, if I regret anything then first it would be only that I failed at what I promised to myself would be done, though I did try but in the end it was not enough. And second, I regret ever to have considered you a brother, when in the time I needed you you chose instead to feel nothing and to leave me all alone, and now won't you go away, for I wish to never see your face again.". And so she said, though her voice betrayed uncertainty hid in those words, and a half-secret wish that he would not leave her there. And hearing these secret words her brother was again moved, and with his strength he rolled the stony gate aside and faced her there. But what he saw was her shining face gone deathly blue and patchy white, and her golden hair was now all come away in clumps, and the sight of her so repulsed him that he turned his back to her and let the stone fall thunder back into its place.

"Ah Sister, why couldn't you have been a little more like me? Then all this trouble could have been avoided. But now like these little humans you have also tasted death, and so I cannot be involved with you any more."

And in the end he sang these words:

i am that i am, ca nèhuātl in nèhuātl
àmo tèhuātl, and you are not

àmo ninomiquitlani

we shall not meet again

Like Yahweh from Asherah, he leaves her there. Takes claim of all the sky to be his own. And so the tandem brother was indeed like a father. The tandem sister was indeed now an other. And it had become conceivable, that something should be lost forever. A loving heart maintains a family, but it is indifference that breaks it, hairline fractures soon eroded till the pieces no longer align. Heaven is far, the earth above her, suffocation, empty lungs, and in those caves, in those far-below caves. In that night, in that blackest of nights. To those fears, to those run-away fears, she soon succumbs.

手

2f

「helló—? 誰かいませんか〜?」

who can it be?, comes knocking at my door
knock-knocking at my door

a human man, thinks he has any right to enter here

this place, it is my home

i will not give it up

30

the man appears outside our door one day, i see him waiting,
knocks and knocks and then stares in through the mail slot,
eyes looking kind-but-also-concerned, how did he find us here,
has seen, it must have been, at night and followed me, well
that's no mind, just wait and he will leave in time, the strange
woman says and with conviction, but i'm not so sure

. . .

poking curiosity, his and mine alike, and his persistence has
me thinking of him even we're alone, and now i feel the time
is passing like i wouldn't have before and make excuses, cut
away back to the door and check to see . . . ah well

. . .

come again, the man is there in winter, and though we haven't
any snow, but still the desert gets quite cold in its emptiness,
and if there had been any water then it surely would have
frozen, and so i cannot help but leave for him, a flask of cinna-
mon tea, because the image, even if it isn't true, of this man is

out there shivering and it's account of us is just too strong to be ignored, and when i duck out in the morning, just before it's time for bed, i see the flask is there and empty, and beside it he's left a note of gratitude

. . .

days are one the next, our cacti flower at odd hours, sometimes for a day or two and sometimes open only night and only briefly, come the bats with fluffy noses spread their seed, feels as if there is an order to the world, and the man a regularity i cannot well remember life without, here each day he brings a little spread of something fits the season, satumaimo in winter becomes ichigo in spring, and then he frowns away a paper and a pen of proper ink, beautiful writing, loops of steady-handed flow, says it's all to be a story he is writing, in the notes we pass to each other, under the gap beneath the door, and the story is a secret but that when it has been finished i can read it, so he says, and if i did he would be very glad of it

and the woman says i'd better quit it now before it's late, and that you'll realise when you're older, exchanging words with such a man, but then i think it's maybe very late already, and that's something to be feared i'm not so sure

31

* she reads a book of underground...

> hmm, speleology, なるほど name

< speleo- stem is what?

> 洞窟のこと, like spelunking

< oh, スペランカー

< video game

> yeh yeh, though first i think 洞窟物語

< ah 君らしい, cute canid creatures

> hehehe

* ...

> u—, thinkin

> cave divers って知ってる？

< うん？

> 水中 spelunkin

> recently i've seen a dream like

> 悪夢 rather, like

> cave-diving and alone, 二人でしなきゃ stuff なのに, and under far gets tether lost, can't find a way back out

> dark water, 潰されて...

* ...

> まあ、ただの夢だけどね

* ...

< ヨシヨシ

32

isn't it dangerous, to let one's self can be subsumed, made a part of someone's someone then by someone you'll be used, and isn't it what i wanted here in this empty world, was a place to be apart and rest, but now this agitation then can we never get away?, then should cut it now before i've been so caught as can't escape and he has everything and i am gone again

.　.　.

and he arrives to find she isn't there

and he waits and waits, and still she isn't there

he looks around the empty space to see a slip of paper says "i am no longer living, so don't worry to wait for me, but take yourself into account, and please take care"

drop the paper fluttering, turns to face the cave again, tightening of muscle, draws a breath he says: "君も人間だろう！"

he says: "come back..."

.   .   .

enter into underland, behind the stone and down down down,
looking for the girl he wants to know

future tense, not a figure built of fictive memories, but to know
her where she stands, though he knows it cannot be done

each we in this world are shadows in the minds of many others
cast projections to compressions, puppet dancing, pull the strings
anger at "the real" diverging from our pet automata
trade anisomorphisms, interfog

well, this is so, then how should we be coupled?

couple tightly is a binding to the model in his mind
is to move-you-by-his-strings

couple loosely is to float away ungrounded
without someone other watching is no spectre left at all

but if we instead idealise a realistic method
keep our symmetries aligned, and with our bitrates opened wide
each our shadows grow just brighter
as we pull a little tighter
into subsets made improper, make a single something new

the you inside of me is now the me inside of you

and, though he knows it cannot be done

but he will try

and he comes to where i've hidden, under rock and over bone,
puts a hand out beckoning

i say "why should i come, if there is no one wants me there?"

"i want you".

he says to me.

that girl who had been running ukifune, drift-away, here it is
she comes back to the shore again,
ただいま
welcome back ^^

33

Lightning, fire and flame. A storm is brewing up on mount Olympus, where Zeus and Hera are, as always, in dispute.

"It was your turn for the garbage", Hera says. "Because you skipped last week and . . . always up to me, holding this family together . . . wouldn't hurt you to try helping out"

"You know you never said anything about . . . supposed to know when you don't actually say . . . sick of the never-ending mind games"

". . . really not that hard . . . try using your brain . . . even Hestia said. . . ."

And on it lasts, for hours and days: waves of insults, exposition, pains, and earnest pleas, until at last there is a temporary lull, and they find they have agreed upon a fair and honest way for the argument to be resolved.

Since neither wishes to be the first to yield, they will take their complaints instead to the goddess Kannon, who will act as mediator. Kannon the merciful and wise, she who takes our pain into herself and gives us healing rest. These two know she will listen without bias and that her answers will be pure.

And so it is they do, descend from the mountain in an uncomfortable silence and to the little cave at its base, where Kannnon stays so that her human visitors may come to her more readily. It is an empty place, with rough stone walls and only a few woven mats for sitting and a candle that never goes out, and there the lady Kannon waits, and on her face a subtle smile, one that seems more a smile of caring than of knowing.

For a moment the two Olympians are silent, waiting for their host to speak. Then, realising what it is she expects, they both begin at once, cutting over one another in a rush.

Hera: "whenever I try to talk with him"

Zeus: "it never comes out right"

Hera: "I don't know if it's me or if"

Zeus: "she never understands"

Hera: "so come now, lady Kannon"

Zeus: "since you have experienced either side"

Hera: "then of women"

Zeus: "and of men"

both: "in caring for the other and indulging in their ways, which of us is the most long-suffering?"

They take a moment to calm themselves and then look to

her expectantly, holding their breaths. And the lady Kannon,
our lady in white, she answers the two of them thus:

men and women, boys and girls
both have grievances
suffered long

fish and dragon, in the lake
stirring up the mud
battle-throng

points of reference contradict
ever failing to predict
mirror-hall illusion, looking out is looking in

but if you look more closely
yin within the yang
light within the dark
you will find it in your heart
clonal colony

walk the root you share
leave your feelings there
fickle pair
two trees sprouting, and they grow
from a common source

"And so, if you are only willing to try a little longer, and to
keep the thoughts of others before your own, then I'm certain
it will all be right in the end. Now come, look at each other,

and lets hear what you have to say."

And these two jealous gods, for the first time in quite a while, they look to one another a little more directly and they try to understand.

34

the boy-from-afar comes visit me in hoozdo, this land of very-
hot. it was 122°F (that's 50°C) just yesterday where we are
now, next to a giant black radiator of igneous rock sucks up
the sun and thermal glowing all through day and into night

we go to see the house where i was grown

the empty house a shell gone hatched has nothing left to give,
only stories, little people, younger faces, wrinkles gone, find
the worn-down-spots and contrast-shades where living used
to be

hidden geographies, buried dogs and citrus trees

and further histories, the people who lived here before, lived
right where i am sitting now, broken pots that once held trea-
sures, trading turquoise and cacao, those people who are called
"exhausted", drew the desert up in lines

there is a rock with petroglyphs, i played on it when small,
with art from 13 hundred years ago and i am only 5

the drawings look like this:

lines on the rocks control the world, art as ritual, lines in the
dust run water, mark out houses, cities, sense of place

their houses built in layers, dig one out over the other, carry
families in living lines, a history in space

but we will not stay in this house

we will give it away and go live Someplace Else.

•   •   •

back at my apartment in the morning, and there comes a little
rain that is so gentle, washes out the dusty sky. my loved-
one is making us breakfast, toufu hamburger, and i pour the
sparkling wine

his clock is still all turned around to 22 at night

so we sleep the morning away

seventh month and seventh day and we are here together,

though it's rainy, but for us a summer's rain is not a thing that
separates

is a gift

we hang our wish from the palo verde because sasa don't grow
in the desert

35

日の出の来る前に
想ひ出の火で
温まった

日の出が来た後は
彼氏の身体^{からだ}に
燃えられた

楽の種育て
ものすごく元気で
すくすくすく
すぐ咲いた

ある日
彼氏
comes to me, says he:
夜を過ごしたり
今度、一緒に

resting under a crooked mesquite, bare feet and khaki shorts, my legs stretched out in front turned bronze and starting to peel, nails reflecting ruby red the sun peeks in between the thorns and tiny leaves, and shifting shadows back and forth across we're munching onigiri, this with takuan vinegar tang and nori salt, finger-pick out of the ice-packed tupperware we made together earlier, at the counter top, working with our hands all four in easy unison, and he leans back against the concrete of the wash to stare the canopy above is hanging beans all going yellow, i answer un, that people grind those up and make them into breads . . . wanna try?

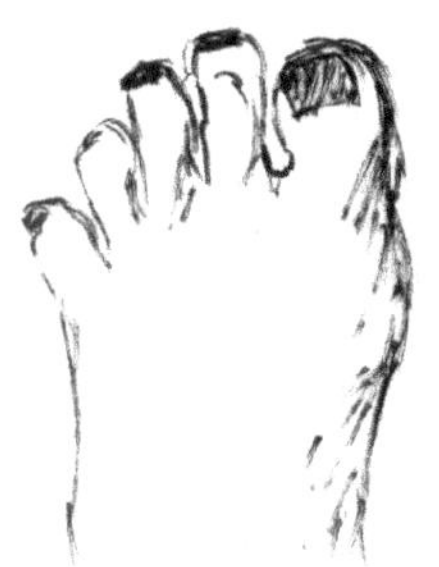 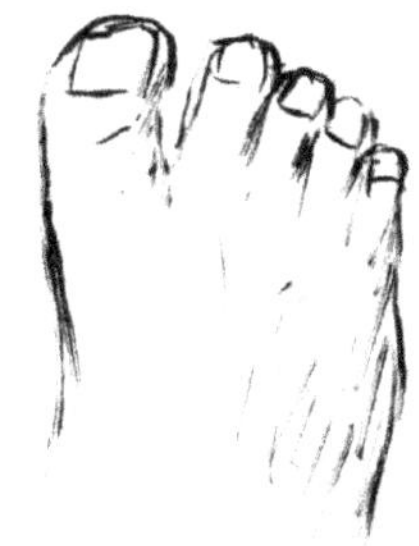

37

"Ok then, just one more. Then this one is about Coyote, and the Sun and the Moon"

凍死した地球

Wooow, boy it's such a hot day today isn't it?

He makes a face, mimes wiping sweat, and all the children laugh

Yeah huh, it sure is hot. But you know, and now maybe you won't even believe it could be true but it is, that there was a time once it used to never get hot at all, all year, not even a little. In fact back then it was cold, freezing cold all over the world, and it lasted that way for years and years. And it's all because that was the time when Sun and Moon had both gone far away, and when the Earth was lost in the dark.

Sun and Moon had quarrelled with each other, and because they both of them were so proud and thought it was the other was at fault they had found it impossible to reconcile with one another. And so Moon had gone high off into the sky to a height where nobody could see him, and Sun had gone deep underground and wouldn't come out again. And, with the two of them gone, the Earth and all its people found that they were in a real mess.

コヨーテの窮まり

And now I said this story would also have Coyote in it, and so here she is:

As you can see, she is quite thin. Coyote hadn't eaten in a while, and the cold of this world gone dark was starting to get at her. Her hair was patchy-shedding from malnutrition, and her feet were numb and blue, and just in general she looked a real mess (though without Sun and Moon around no one could see her very well, for which she was grateful, in a sad sort of way).

But our story starts when this has all gone on a little while already, and Coyote now was wandering, in a sort of haze all given up, shut off from her body and its hunger and without thought or care, which is called dissociation, like those monks in funny clothes like to do when they all sit around for hours and stare at a wall (as if that was supposed to be something fun to do, hah. And if either of you start to feel like that, or like you're really tired and it's getting hard to care, well then you just come to me and let me know, ok? Cause I'm always here to help.) And so Coyote she was wandering along, shuffling her feet and hanging tail and not at all looking ahead at where she's going, until . . . *bonk*:

She ran face-first into a big old rock and fell back on her haunches, stunned. And that impact woke her up to knowing something had to be done. "I must find the Sun and bring her back to the sky!", Coyote thought. "Or else soon I will starve. Because without her around it's impossible to hunt, and I keep stubbing my nose against all these rocks and trees that I can't see." And so Coyote got up determined and went out searching, moving slowly and keeping her nose to the dust to search for Sun's smell, which is like the smell of laundry hung to dry on a bright midsummer day.

And so she searched and she searched, and she got hungrier and hungrier, until at last she came around again to that very same rock, and curled up next to it, feeling tired and dejected. And like that she fell asleep.

不思議な盟約

Coyote slept there for a long time, so exhausted and without a sun to wake her up again, because you know our bodies rhythms are linked to the sun as it comes and goes, and without that cycle of light to remind it what time it is we can fall out of sync with the world and sleep and wake at the oddest hours (which for kids like you is not healthy because you're still growing, see? So be sure you shut out the light when your parents ask you to).

But anyways so Coyote slept, and she would have kept on doing if it wasn't for a certain clever someone came to wake her up again.

"Ba:pt o hi: Coyote?, out travelling when it's so dark this way.", said Usagi, who was perched up on the rock above her head. "Isn't it dangerous? And wow but don't you look an awful sight. How long has it been since you last ate?" (or took a bath?, he thought but tactfully didn't add).

"Ohoh, it's little Usagi! And but isn't this brave of you to approach me so, even if I am in a such a state. Tell me then, why shouldn't I eat you up right now?, seeing as you look so tasty and, as you say, I'm feeling *so* very hungry." And Coyote gave him a weak, smirking sort of smile.

Usagi's nose twitched, but only a little. "Oh Coyote, you're so clever of course you can guess why, and anyways I'm so small that even if you ate me up you'd be hungry again in an instant, and what we both need is instead to find a way to bring back Sun to this world so that new food can grow again and we can keep on living for the longer term. And you see, what I've got is a plan for how we two can do just that."

And Coyote was already convinced, cause she could see he wasn't lying, but she kept up the dangerous act a little longer cause she liked how Usagi reacted to it, and asked, "well tell me then, little one, what plan is this you have for us?".

"Well see, alone I don't think we can find where Sun has gone to hide, but Moon was there when all this happened and must know where she's gotten off to. And anyways I doubt she would come out without him there, because that's how the two of them used to work, you know?, always together. But to get to him we've got to reach a certain special place, and that's why I need your help. Because what you can do comes from where you are, and where you are comes from what you can do, and what *you* can do, with that nose of yours, is to lead us up through to the heart of the mountain maze, and from there I'll show you what it is *I* can do. Though first you must promise me just one thing, which is that if we succeed in this then you will never eat meat again, and that way we can live together happily." And to this Coyote agreed, thinking "we may as well give it a try, and I always can just break the promise later if I feel like it", and that was that.

So Usagi led, and Coyote, though feeling dubious, she followed, biting back questions she was certain that her new ally wouldn't answer. And together up they climbed the side of the muhaḍagĭ du'ag (which is how back then they called our own 南山, you know, although at that time it wasn't city around and only saguaro and creosote were there to see them going). And about halfway up is where they reached the entrance to the dangerous mountain maze.

Now neither of those two knew it, but what was special about this maze is this, that if someone's motivated by greed or wanting things to have alone, then that person is going to get lost and never find a way back out again. And you know that's how Coyote used to be, a little greedy and always acting out and looking for ways like that to get ahead. But this time she was working together with Usagi, and though she still wasn't quite certain that he could be trusted, but she really did want this all to work out and was feeling secretly glad that she'd finally found a friend, and so because of that when Coyote sniffed ahead leading Usagi through the maze, well it saw that she was earnest and the maze let the two of them through.

And, when they came at last to its very heart, the maze opened up again, and they found themselves at the mountain's summit, on a pile of rocks turned shining manganese-black (or else they would have done with Sun around to show it). And Usagi did a happy little dance, hopped up a rock, pulled out his flute, and he poised himself to play.

"This trick I learned from S-e'ehe, though he did not know I was watching."

tiwiwiwiwiwiwiwiwiwi～

towowowowowowowowo～

The sound from his flute had a strange sort of carry to it I can't well describe that let it spread far and wide without growing any louder than was comfortable to hear. And when Coyote heard it she knew that from way up here Moon surely must hear it as well, and so he did, and came down to meet them there.

嘘の女・箱に入らない女

"Oh Coyote you false! Of course it's you who would deceive me so to bring me down to earth. Well then, let's hear what you have got to say."

And Coyote felt a little sheepish that Moon attributed to her the trick that really was Usagi's, but she was clever as well and all this while been thinking of what to say to him and began with a little speech she had composed.

"每日每日 we:s taṣ, oh Moon don't you ever feel lonesome? To float up there and nobody else around, don't you know the world has moved on to the greater vehicle and that there's no need any longer to deprive yourself this way? Wouldn't you rather have someone else to talk with you? And Sun is alone as well, I'm sure that after all this time she would be glad to hear from you again. It used to be you were so close, and it's a pity such a little difference should get between the two of you, and for all this time it's been."

"Coyote, you aloner, what can you know of the trouble that comes between women and men? And in the first place it's not me who started this. 'Am 'o me: hegai uvĭ ñ I've been here all this time alone. Pi 'o ke:k hegai uvĭ, and you cannot raise the dead. Though I only wanted the best for her, but she chose not to hear me instead, and she put herself into that state all by herself. And it's always me who has to be the reasonable one. . ."

"But Moon, even if she acted alone, is it so wrong to go to her? Can't we compromise to meet the ones we love?"

"Why is it that only *she* should be freed while *I* am still constrained?"

"Are you constrained?", asked Usagi.

"By these expectations that have been placed on me, I am constrained. That is how things are in this world!, that living we must keep our cool and not let anything get to us."

"Must it be so?", asked Coyote.

"Well it's just naturally so! Everyone knows it must be so!"

"Is that true? Does everyone know that it must be so?", asked they both, and Moon's certainty began to waver.

And it took them a while longer, but in the end Moon was convinced, and he felt sorry for the way he had behaved, which was to leave the one who loved him in the time she needed him most. And maybe that wouldn't be so hard a thing to admit for two little ones like you, but you see when you start getting older it becomes more difficult, and you start to get more stubborn, and so for somebody like Moon it was the hardest thing of all, and well worth telling a story about.

こいこいでてこい

So Moon led them all to the place where Sun had hidden herself away, which was inside a pitch black cave with a big stone rolled across its entrance.

And next what they decided to do was to go about and gather together all the animals who were living there, because they too would be just as affected by the darkness and desperate about seeing Sun again. And once everybody was gathered together they thought it was best to have everyone go in turns at trying to call Sun out of her cave, as each one of them had something different to say.

Two quail were there and cooed about how it's no good to be alone, and everyone should have a partner to depend on. And a javelina then spoke up to say just two was not enough, and really everyone should live in groups of four or five or six, because you can get chores done much more quickly that way.

But Sun's voice came up from the cave saying "why should I need anyone? I am strong all on my own and have fought hard for this liberation. All things in this world evolve and grow, and to rely on others is a hindrance to this process, to subject oneself to others is to be tied down and forced into apoptosis. No, I think I am quite alright, living alone.".

"But sister, are you really living at all?", asked a pronghorn munching, "when without our symbionts we could not even digest our food, I thought to live is always to rely on others".

But again Sun was not moved, and replied "well, if you say that to be alone is also to be dead, then maybe I prefer this death over the chains of 'womanliness' that social structures put on me. This way at least I can be just myself and not be anyone else.".

And next an ageha who had fluttered down and landed on a clump of brittlebush began to speak, though she was so quiet hardly anyone could hear her, but I heard, and she said "don't you know, i too have died before and come to life again, and living is so much better now here on the other side, flying freely with these colourful wings of mine".

And there came a few more questions, and some more annoyed replies, until all the animals began speaking up and making noise at once, and it got to be quite a racket. And little Naṣkel was there too, and mad that nobody payed him attention, so he went around stinging ankles and making people jump and howl, and the crowd all toppled over each other into a wiggling pile (which looked a lot like you two actually when you're out there rolling around in the yard, and after this you both have got to take a bath, alright? No buts).

And the noise had got so bad that Sun came out just to see what all the trouble was. But at that moment she saw Moon there, who looked her squarely in the eyes, and for the two of them all the noise and hubbub seemed to die away. And silently Moon mouthed the words "I'm sorry", and Sun said "I'm sorry too", and the two of them from that point on knew somehow they would get along again, though there would likely be more problems in the future, but whatever happened they would work it out. And that's just the way it's been.

黄泉がえり

So Sun and Moon came back into the world, and it was thanks to that unlikely pair of friends, Usagi and Coyote, whom no one would have believed could get along so well. And all four of them, to celebrate their friendship, spent the day together and drank wine of ha:ṣañ until they were dizzy and stumbling and felt a little ill, but very happy and glowing red. And hearing laughter come from the two celestial bodies was enough to wake up Wind Man where he slept, which was on a mountain that's some ways off to the west from here, and he turned to his partner, who was still curled up and sleeping, kicked him in the ribs, and said "wake up; we've got some work to do".

And this is the part I'm sure you both know, so why don't you tell me then? Tell me what is it that happens when it's smack in the middle of summer and so hot, and there's sweat collecting down your chest and your eyes are squinted shut.

But then you start to feel a change coming on, and you start to get that feeling like your body feels *so* light and like the whole world is expanding, and there's just a little wind goes rustle rustle, and your head so light like it's floating up up up into the sky, tell me what does it mean is going to happen next?

That it's going to rain!!

Mmm hmm, that's what it means, and the steps of it go like this, that first you're feeling so much lighter, and the world a little brighter with this glow comes of diffraction when there's moisture in the air. And you feel yourself start smiling, though at this point maybe you're still not quite sure why. Then comes next is the wind, shaking up stale summer air, and the trees will start to wave and hair is blown into your eyes, and your body starts to dance all on its own. Then the dust rolls in a wave, turns all the world a martian orange, oxidation and a taste leaks in between your lips and lashes till you've got no choice but to hide, and some trees might lose their branches, and it's red red red, till the sky starts going dark.

And then at last you hear the kami nari, gods cry out a song together as they work, bringing life back to the world. And this is all because the Sun and Moon are here, that we can have the rain, because without them all the winds and waves would give up moving and settle down to stillness, and the rivers wouldn't run, and the land would all be empty, dry, and dark. But thanks to Usagi and Coyote working together, even though everyone thought they rightly should be enemies, it's thanks to them that we can have our world alive again, and so be sure you thank them well by making friends with even your greatest enemies and try your hardest first to work things out. Because, from that, good things will come.

結局、女性は太陽になった

In the end, woman was the Sun. Or maybe it's the Moon. The two are now so tangled, and they share their light so freely, that whenever one is shining the other is there as complement, and between them earth is never left alone.

The well-lit earth is fertile, plants and fungi overgroweth. A world wound round in webs, of photic plankters, ocean snow. Painted green (or red or brown), take light and spread it, thin-diffracted, fill our veins up with negentropy, respire and flow away. And in the brand new day that hungry Coyote begins to eat like she's never eaten before, ravenous, like she's afraid the lights will all go out again and that this meal will end up both her first and last. She hunts mashua and chilis, tomatillo green and tart, kinkan, grapefruit, grapes and olives, round and full. And when she's all filled up that banmakam stretches a long, contented yawn, plops down a shady spot, fawump, and gives a prayer to Ukemochi for the feast.

And she begins to sing:

we are here not long, not long
briefly on the earth
so let us eat and drink our fill
ohuaya ohuaya

wither-trees and broken-wings
sing! flower-and-song
let us labour in the sun
ohuaya oe–

完

[end]

人間仲間

some people helped a lot with this book, and i am very grateful:

- sensei who said "try it" when i still felt all uncertain
- rose is a rose, i'm really glad you're here
- loved one helps me always in too many ways to mention
- my sister is encouraging, even when things are weird

to you and more, i wanna say: ❤

rain of long time is a small, independent press started by me (ageha) with the goal of publishing my own books alongside certain things from the public domain which ought not to be forgotten.

its focus is on prose works that incorporate aspects of poetry or themes of outsidership, the fantastic, or multiculturalism.

another side-goal of this project is to delegitimise the idea of intellectual property, and so accordingly all books are shared under some combination of creative commons licensing and public domain availability, with digital copies in pdf format also freely available for download.

more books can be found here: https://rain-of-long-time.com

thank you

for reading ^^